MEDITERRANEAN

WARSCAPES

pSet
Press, inc.

2018

Copyright © Warscapes Magazine 2018
First edition
ISBN: 978-1-937357-98-6

Warscapes magazine is grateful for the generous support of
Alessandro d'Ansembourg, the Kahane Foundation,
Compton Foundation, and UpSet Press.

COVER & BOOK DESIGN
Shiman Shan

ART & PHOTOGRAPHY CREDITS
Mario Badagliacca, Frammenti, 10 images courtesy the artist, 2017.
Mujtaba Jalili, De Koepel Prison, 2 images courtesy the photographer, 2017.
Intermundia documentation photos copyright © Ana Dana Beroš and
Stjepan Žgela, 2014.
Intermundia interior photos copyright © Ana Dana Beroš, 2014.
"Earth Paradise" photograph copyright © Dinko Cepak, 2013.
"Here and There" photography copyright © Ana Mihalić, 2013.
"Taka" photography copyright © Kate Stanworth, 2016.
"Ahmed" photography copyright © Hassan Ghedi Santur, 2015.
"The Gift" photography copyright © Alfredo Jaar, 2016.

Warscapes Magazine
95 Bundy Lane
Storrs, CT 06268

www.warscapes.com

PRINTED IN THE UNITED STATES OF AMERICA.

edited by

Bhakti Shringarpure
Michael Busch
Michael Bronner
Veruska Cantelli
Melissa Smyth
Jessica Rohan
Gareth Davies
Jason Huettner
Noam Scheindlin

Warscapes Magazine and UpSet Press

Contents

Where are your monuments, your battles, martyrs?
Where is your tribal memory? Sirs,
in that grey vault. The sea. The sea
has locked them up. The sea is History.

"The Sea is History," Derek Walcott

black and blues

Boubacar Boris Diop

An expanse of blue. Flickering through black and white images. A black hole of memory. Fragile and visible only because of its absence. It might be a village but it's set deep in the heart of the city. Almost a *trompe-l'oeil*. The sea, with its cruel double standards, devours the bodies as much as it nurtures them.

Césaire would have said: houses *eerily stranded* on the beach. A tire wedged between the pebbles and the algae. Fragments of a broken bottle scattered around a sandy mound, a beach cluttered with all sorts of detritus. One must tread carefully on the beach, to avoid cuts from the shards or stains from the excrement. The ocean, though close by, is inaccessible, relentlessly taking back what it gives mankind. It is hard to imagine what type of life would be possible in such a place.

Here, all social activities revolve around fishing. In swift, skillful moves that hark back to the dawn of time, young men wind their ropes in preparation for the imminent journey. Women lean over stalls dotted with stray heaps of sea bass. They're not just sorting out the day's catch, picking out some to be dried under the sun and others to be salted: they are also counting these little treasures from the sea. Without these life would be worse.

These men of the sea know it instinctively: fishing nets draw worlds closer to each other weaving a link between here and faraway. If only because of this ability to connect everything, one feels inclined to compare them to the boats you see, or rather imagine, are everywhere. Perhaps that was the case before. *Before*: what exactly does this word mean? It was such a long time ago, in a previous life. Today, it's hard to think there was a time when boats weren't possessed by the sea, a time when they symbolized life, not death.

If only you dare to open your eyes. The village has been depleted of its menfolk. How strange it is to stand on the seashore facing the foaming, surging waves, and yet be able to only think of the desert. Children are squeezed in a boat and some are surprised to find themselves wondering whether they are learning how to fish or learning to map the route to the Balearic Islands or Lampedusa at the risk of death. They don't know themselves but on their haggard faces you can clearly see that it has been a long time since their body and spirit were a single entity.

In the pictures, only the women's eyes don't have a faraway look. The women stare down at the ground to hide their distress. They can't picture themselves living anywhere but in these tiny, humble dwellings wedged between car repair shops and food stalls. They did nothing to hold onto their sons, for they are men and—as the saying goes—it's unbecoming for a man worthy of his name to resign himself to destitution and medi-ocrity. Like their fathers, they have done well to leave even though at the end of the day this running away, ever further away from themselves, hasn't been good for anyone. Surely one can't expect the matriarch to resign herself to such a separation with a light heart. You can easily read on their beautiful ebony faces how much *they too* suffer from the fact that so many places, real or barely conceivable, are engaged in a dark battle for precedence over their minds. Even as they look into the lens—graciously but without really being present—they are serious and impenetrable but most of all, alone.

As the setting sun is reflected onto the surface of the water, the closing lines of those delirious nocturnal stories of old come to mind: "And here I let the tale vanish into the sea, and the first to smell its fragrance will go to Paradise!" And yet in this topsy-turvy world, it is only at such a parting moment that the tale truly unfolds in its full splendor. Under the gaze of a little black and yellow creature—a tiny speck on the vast, blue expanse of the Atlantic—stands a house in ruins, its heart gnawed by sea-salt, neigh-ing and galloping into the night. The ocean becomes a lake, and the lake a mirror, reflecting the returning shadows of those who left. Neither men nor women, they are timeless beings: dark lines hovering over the sea.

Do they dream of setting out on a journey home?

Taka. Photo by Kate Stanworth.

Postcard from Sicily

Ismail Einashe

Most weekday afternoons on the seafront in La Kalsa, a historic district of Palermo near the city's harbor, young African migrants gather in groups to play football. Around them, Sicilians go about their daily lives. A mother pushes a pram through the crowds; two women practice yoga on a floral rug; children fly kites high in the air; stray dogs roam in the distance; and young Italians queue up to buy cold granitas in the sweltering June sun. Along the promenade in the evenings, Nigerian women trafficked into prostitution sell their bodies for twenty-five euros, while up the road, Chinese massage parlors charge a little more. Nearby, a few tourists sit on tables outside restaurants tucking into clam pasta.

It is here that I meet Taka, a seventeen-year-old from Gambia. He has a slender, tall frame, his whole being radiant with a huge smile that reveals a set of perfect teeth. When he landed in Palermo last year, the Italian coastguard asked him, "What is your age?" Because he was only seventeen, he was put into a reception center for minors a thirty-minute walk from the city center. Those first few days, he said, he walked the streets with a big smile on his face. The police would ask him why he was smiling. He told them, "Because I am happy. In Africa, to be in Europe is a big thing."

Looking at his delicate frame, I am reminded of my cousin Abdi, who made his own journey across the Mediterranean Sea at the age of fourteen. He left Hargeisa, in Somaliland, one day without telling my Aunt Anab where he was going. When I last saw my aunt, she told me that, "He came to me one morning and asked me for a dollar. I told him I didn't have any money, and then he left." My aunt cried for her son but he turned up some days later in

Ethiopia, saying he needed to pay smugglers to get him to Europe. Abdi is now living in Austria, but he may not be able to stay once he turns eighteen. As I sit here with Taka, I wonder if he thought much about what happens to young migrants like him after they arrive in Europe. A young Gambian I recently met in a small town in Basilicata—a region between Puglia and Calabria—said to me, "The journey is like taking a penalty shot: Either you get the ball in, or you don't." Luckily for Taka and my cousin, they got the ball in. Yet their lives are currently in limbo.

For me, Europe is a strange place to be. I work as a reporter in places like Sicily, but I also have family members who have made these dangerous journeys across the Mediterranean, a sea that has taken so many lives. Last year it swallowed 5,000 souls.

Most of these young men playing football on this field are supported by a local charity in Palermo, which provides them with a kit, a ball and a referee. They gather in this green field between a road and the sea. Most are from West Africa—Gambians, Nigerians and Senegalese, among others. For several weeks last summer, I was in Palermo researching the experiences of recently arrived African migrants. I got to know several of these young men. Their daily sessions of football and dreaming of becoming the next African soccer star in Europe gave them a measure of solace in an otherwise bleak struggle faced by young African migrants in Sicily. What is often a life in limbo here is marked by cycles of isolation, poverty and boredom.

When I met Taka he showed little fear, and mostly enthusiasm. His friend Landi, on the other hand, was more crafty and wary of my foreignness. Strangely, these young teens fre-quently send me WhatsApp messages, things like, "I miss you dear," or "How are you my dear?" I tried to explain to them that using "dear" like this is sounds strange in English. Somehow, my suggestions have been lost in translation. On my birthday last year, Taka sent me a note he recorded in which he called me "dear."

Sometimes I don't hear from Taka for a long time. Then suddenly a WhatsApp message will arrive: "Hello dear I have been thinking about you, I miss you." He tells me what he has been up to. He's still in Sicily waiting for what comes next, but his friend Landi has since resettled in Germany. As yet, Taka has not been signed by a football team like he dreamed of, but he seems happy nonetheless. Like so many young African migrants I know, Taka and his friends love posting selfies and group photos of them-selves online. I sometimes follow the comments made at the bottom of their posts and see these young men, most of whom still appear to be back in their countries, commenting, "You look beautiful in Europe."

Back to La Kalsa. The sun is setting behind the rolling hills that circle the city; well-healed Italians sit on the terraces of the restaurants having an aperitif while joggers run along the promenade. The football session is coming to an end, and Taka is clearing up for the day. His yellow t-shirt is covered in mud. He has the half-hour walk ahead of him to the reception center for young migrants, where he still resides. There, he sleeps in a communal block and survives on ten euros a week. Sicilians don't speak English, and they eat pasta. Taka complains, "I don't like the taste. I hate it."

For the most part, though, Taka is a happy teen content to walk in the sunshine and wish away the dark corners of his memory. Yet sometimes, those memories of nights spent living in Tripoli haunt him. He tells me that, "Libya is a bad place. You have to stick together in Tripoli or

you get kidnapped." Sometimes these young, kidnapped men get sold into slavery. I feel for Taka—he's experienced horrendous levels of fear and insecurity during his young life. His stories of being in Libya during its civil war remind me of my own childhood in Somalia. Those days were full of fear and adrenalin. Like Taka, his friends Papi and Kadim are both seventeen years old and from Gambia. They share similar stories with me. When they arrived in Palermo, their happiness quickly gave way to the realization of how hard life is in Sicily. Kadim, wearing a cap, a gold chain and sportswear, tells me that life in Sicily is really not much that better than in Africa. Indeed, locals here frequently joke that Sicily is a country in Africa.

Jokes aside, Taka has no time for regret. And yet, as more young migrants like Taka arrive on the island, the situation becomes increasingly tense. His friends on Facebook still comment that, "You look nice dear." And it's true—he's looking good in Europe. Taka tells me that his friends had warned him not to make the journey. They told him the dangers were all too real. "I thought they were lying to me," he says. "Now I know what they meant."

THE WATER

To Bassem and Doa, for their love,
and their bravery.
For the one of them who drowned.

(Tell It)

The Water carried my body.
The Water didn't carry body, it was
my body
carried
the Water.

(Tell It)

When the sea is calm, the boats keep coming,

When the summer ends, the boats don't stop.

Shipwrecks begin.

(Tell It)

Malta mon amour, how many shoeless bodies
at the bottom of the sea?

(Tell It)

Sublimation is when solid turns to gas,
without becoming liquid
I wish I died like that, without becoming Water.

Jehan Bseiso

REFUGEE STATUS DETERMINATION

Part 1

Morning show hostess is wearing matte red lipstick
The color is Russian Red (by Mac).

She says:
"There are 65 million refugees around the world,
this is the highest number ever recorded."

Ever

The new #Ikea tent comes in colors like:

"Aleppo Sunrise"

 and

"Lifejacket Orange"

"It has everything they need" says the TV
but home,

(please, please, please open the border)
I haven't seen my mother since 2011,
            I forgot how to play the piano,
                    I want to tell him I love him,
I have diabetes and I will die without Insulin,

(please, please, please open the border)

Part Two

The march on Washington starts from Occupied
Jerusalem.

This is how we refugee.

Jehan Bseiso

Sambus

Hamdi, Somalia

Ingredients

1 kg of ground beef
250 grams of flour
1 white onion
A pinch of black pepper
1 tablespoon of cumin or curry
1 teaspoon of salt
1 litre of oil for frying
Water as necessary
Parsley (to your liking)

Preparation (for 4 people)

The dough:
Mix and knead the flour with water and salt. Stretch out the dough in the form of a disk as if making a pizza, as thin as possible. Cut through the disk with two crossing diagonal lines to obtain four triangular parts.

The filling:
In a frying pan, cook the ground beef together with the chopped onion, pepper and salt until the meat is nice and brown. Then add cumin or curry and the parsley just a few minutes before taking it off the burner.

Stir a tablespoon of flour in a glass of water to be used as glue. It should be neither dense nor liquid. Create cones with the triangular dough and fill them with some of the spiced ground beef, gluing the corners with the flour mixture. Fry the sambus in very hot vegetable oil, turning them over every few minutes. They will be ready once they reach a golden color (in about 4 minutes).

I remember very well the first time I cooked. I was fifteen years old. My mother didn't want me near the stove or doing any housekeeping. She used to cuddle me and was always afraid of the fire from the burners. But I really loved cooking, so one day while my mother was out and I was alone in the house, I started cooking a meal. When my family returned, everything was ready.

My family is very large, six sisters and three brothers. I studied in a private English school because, since 1990, public schools have not been accessible in Somalia. The war brought destruction and that signaled the end of our life. We could not go out and could not go to school. My brother and his daughter died under the bombs. I remember the desperation of a close friend who returned home to find a pile of rubble under which her entire family lost its life.

We could not stay in Somalia. Those who escaped death fled to other countries. I was terrified and wanted to leave. My mother didn't want me to go, my brother was the one who helped me. I left with some of his friends and my cousin. Everyone was much older than me. I was only seventeen.

I crossed the desert in a 4X4 along with fifty other people. The journey was terrible; it felt almost worse than being under the bombs. After three days, we no longer had food or water. During those months, I often regretted having left, but thankfully I survived.

At the Libyan border, we were kidnapped and taken to a home where we couldn't leave without giving our captors all our money. I told them I didn't have any money and they became angry with me. They could do anything to a woman. I stayed in Libya for a month waiting for my journey to Europe, the dream of all of us, a place where we could have freedom, peace, wealth…

In May 2008, I got on a boat for the first time along with sixty people. There was so much confusion, everyone was screaming as if they had gone mad. We were all shocked not to see a safe boat as expected. Instead, it was a small dinghy, too small for all of us. In the end, we went anyway. On the second day of our journey, the dinghy was already deflating and sinking but thank God we were rescued by a large ship that was nearby and which took us to Tunisia. From there we reached Tripoli by foot. During our journey back to Libya we were afraid to be arrested, we knew it happened to some of us. We cannot travel freely, we do not have a proper visa and we live in constant fear even when we haven't done anything wrong.

After three weeks we were told that we could board another boat to Europe—no one ever knows how long it takes for that to happen. You have to wait, wait, wait and hope that in the meantime you will not be kidnapped in the streets, raped, or locked up. Like the previous boat, this one was also very precarious, and this time there were seven children and several pregnant women among the passengers. On the second day of our journey, the boat literally split in half. We all started screaming, crying and praying, but God is mighty and I escaped death this time, too. I remember the rescue team arriving immediately and we were taken to Lampedusa. I still remember the warmth of those who came to help us at the port.

After few days I was taken to Bari to a camp where there were almost two thousand people. They put me in a container along with two Somali girls. I stayed in that camp for eight months waiting for a hearing with the commission in order to receive my permit to stay. Those eight months were brutal, time seemed to never pass. But then I met my husband, Qader. Actually, we knew each other from when we were in Somalia. He used to come play soccer with my brothers in the neighborhood but we were children then. When we saw each other again in Bari we started to date. He was nice to me, we were both in a precarious situation. He had not yet had his hearing with the commission.

When I left the camp with a permit, I didn't have a place to go. I was alone, in the streets, and so I tried my luck and travelled to Switzerland. Once there, I presented an application for asylum and after three months the police told me I couldn't stay. I was taken to a special jail where all the undocumented foreigners were detained. After a few days, handcuffed, they took me to the airport to board a flight to Rome's Fiumicino airport. Handcuffed… I felt so ashamed! I am not a criminal. I am a young woman looking for peace and tranquility. That is how I returned to Italy.

I was sent to a welcome center in Sicily where I worked as a housemaid for an Italian family. The situation was fine but very precarious. In the meantime, Qader continued to call me and one day he asked me to marry him.

We immediately called our families and they organized a proxy marriage. On the phone, my mother asked me if I was happy with Qader and I replied yes. She cried for my happiness. She had been worried about me, young and alone on this journey. I had just turned eighteen. On the phone with the *qadi* from Mogadishu my husband and I exchanged our vows and our families celebrated together for us in Mogadishu. In Somalia, a wedding is a very special celebration. Those who are wealthy can offer a camel. Our families could offer only four cows and four lambs. Qader and I could not celebrate as we would have liked and I missed not having all my family and friends on that special occasion. I missed the *shaash saar*, the scarves that women give as a gift to a bride after the wedding. Sambus are prepared for this occasion too, along with many sweets while singing and laughing among women. But that's life…

Now I have two children, a girl and a boy. My mother has only met them via photographs, and I am not sure when and if they will ever be able to meet in person. My first child is a girl and she is vivacious and intelligent. I speak to her in Somali and she understands everything though she always replies in Italian. History can be strange. My grandfather spoke Italian and now my daughter speaks it too, but for the opposite reasons. She is beautiful and I would never do to her what they have done to me when I was just a bit older…

I still remember it so vividly. I was at home with my mother waiting for Nadifa, an older woman who "sewed girls." They laid me down and told me that, from that day on, I would become a clean woman and then all I remember was the pain and the fear of dying. I was "sewed" without anesthesia and for two weeks I was very sick in bed. I was afraid to even go to the bathroom. I have escaped death so many times: first as a child, then under the bombs, and twice on the sea.

I will never put my daughter through that experience. Infibulation is a tribal practice that has nothing to do with Islam. I remember that, right before I left Somalia, this was a topic of discussion and even imams used to say that Islam did not mandate infibulation, a tradition that does not need to be respected. Therefore, for Islam, doing so is not a sin. I remember my mother's face when she apologized to me for having put me through it. Even she had started to view it as dangerous and would be happy if it were no longer practiced. I will never do such a thing to my daughter because I love her too much.

I miss my mother very much. I hear her voice while I make sambus for my family. I see her joking, and immediately I become very sad and revisit everything I went through. Often, I cook and eat by myself and cry. In Somalia, it is inconceivable that a person eats by herself. We always eat together, three times a day, for breakfast, lunch and dinner. And we also talk a lot, we tell each other about our day and sometimes we argue.

I call my mother every day. Usually, she laughs, blesses me and tells me not to be worried. But then there are days when she cannot hold her tears because she is afraid she will never see me again. I reassure her and tell her that she will see her grandchildren soon. I make sure to sound cheerful, but as soon as I hang up…

Translated by Veruska Cantelli.
From: *Cum-panis: Storie di fuga, identità e memorie,
in quattro ricette* a cura di Associazione Culturale
Multietnica "La Kasbah Onlus," di Enza Papa e
Francesco Mollo Edizioni Erranti, 2014.

It was born to me of things
that are not of land
of kingdoms and kingdoms
that I had and I lost
of all things living
that I have seen die
of all that was mine
and went from me

"Land of Absence," Gabriela Mistral

Nepenthe

Mazaa Mengiste

One day we will find a language for this. A way to fit it all in the mouth then swallow into the folds of history. There will no longer be the torn photograph, the rusted spoon, the broken cigarettes, the woman's body floating in a sinking boat. That child, face down in the sand, will disappear. Remembering itself, the sea will no longer speak for the sky. Blue will simply turn back to blue. There will be no metaphors, only movement and land and documents and a tongue held still between dulled teeth. I don't want to die in a language I cannot understand: this is Borges descending heavily into the dark stairwell, a library tucked inside his throat. Maybe we know too much. That is the problem that plagued Medea. When Cassandra crossed the placid sea, she knew it was Iphigenia who glanced up, past the waves, and smiled. Kidus Giorgis slayed the dragon but we can still burn in fire. My grandmother warned me. She said, our dreams will bury us then weep. I call out to her now, she who is also named Maaza, she who stands at the shore's edge, muted by time. Who asks to be here, I say. We are split, she says. You have two throats. Beware.

Frammenti

Mario Badagliacca

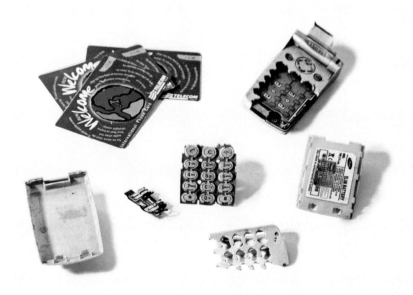

Fragments: An Archaeology Of Dislocation
Veruska Cantelli

October 11, 2013, marks the death and disappearance
of 260 migrants sixty miles off the coast of Lampedusa.
A stain on the conscience of Fortress Europe. One
that keeps unleashing shame as the number of deaths
keeps rising.

Days after the incident, photographer Mario Badagliacca,
in collaboration with Archivio delle Memorie Migranti
(AMM), Progetto Isole and the Askavusa Collective,
began working on recovering objects left behind by
migrants and refugees in crafts now amassed at the
"boat cemetery." Activists from Askavusa Collective
were the first to rescue boxes full of dumped objects
and created a space (Porto M), open to the public,
where people can come and retrace the stories
and journeys of the lives that passed through the
Mediterranean. As part of his work as a documentary
photographer, Badagliacca found himself in an attic
going through those items and seeing "fears, expecta-
tions, and pieces of the life of their owners."

Badagliacca's *Fragments* is not just part of an effort to
mark communal tragedy, the memory of an undistin-
guished multitude to ease our own sense of discomfort
and desire for closure. In each object we are compelled
to see the evidence of a state of mind—not our own.
We look for terror and find it in a muddy object. We find
a glimpse of the quotidian, the reassuring gestures
of handling things. Do these relics speak of a forced
departure?

In their absences, they allow us to imagine bodies, their
story, a relation of attachment, the coexistence of
a silent pact charged with home, continuity, longing,
communality, becoming and violence, chaos, panic,
haste, anxiety, uncertainty, dispersion.

Fragments frame memory. We depend on them to retrieve
steps to rescue forgotten journeys. Badagliacca's
fragments take a life of their own. Away from the material
world, they guide us through a geography of dispersion.
Puncturing our well-practiced ethics, they become
anchors redirecting care toward the singularity of human
struggle. As photographs of crowded boats flood the
media, projecting an undifferentiated understanding of
experience, these fragments propose the arduous journey of undoing accumulation, a thrust toward listening.

Birth

Edwidge Danticat

I felt you reaching out to me that morning. To touch me where the water led you. It's still too hard for me to reach back, cup myself to fill your hand. Bless the resurrection that smells like the sea. But it does not give us a longer moment together. For we are floating on different currents. Our last stroke to eternity. Write me something with your breath, in one of those tongues yet to be heard. They say there will be no country in the future. Twenty-five years and everything will be water and dust. Do you already know the name of that world? Tell me now or whisper it into the wind. They do not know that I'll never make a sound to understand. I'll never see a thing in their world. My mother will never hold me. My father will cry over me. All has been lost, they will say. Evoking their single thread of lineage as though it were made of nations. They will speak of you my whole life. So we should have more than this instant as I enter and you exit. Tell me quickly. What am I to teach them? What am I to learn?

Exile is strangely compelling to think about but terrible to experience. It is the unhealable rift forced between a human being and a native place, between the self and its true home: its essential sadness can never be surmounted.

"Reflections on Exile," Edward Said

JOSS STICKS

I sit and dream
For some dawn still in a tussle
With a deeply entrenched night

Action inaction
To and from
Up and down
Behind beneath and around

Nostalgic bitterness mimics the waft
Of joss sticks made from tamarind
Or mandrake leaves

And the unease—
    Stupendous, swirling—
Is captured in the image
Behind cupped hands

Ali Jimale Ahmed

INCANTATIONS

The walking dead know what wounds they bear

Swirls of incantations rise to an eerie crescendo
As counterpoints of relics on reeds melt at the altar
And ghosts in drabs nudge
Erstwhile adversaries off the edge.

Town criers in civvies herald a dawn of innocence
Castrated by slivers of mutinied stars
Abandoning the hopeful at the dusk-dawn divide.

Hopes, themselves accretions of pastoral years
Ladled from the bosom of fleeting experiences,
Wilt. And cascading straws
Like mirages on horizons
Tantalizing and teasing squinting eyes
Jilt the drowning person.

Ali Jimale Ahmed

Zighinì

Yurdanus, Eritrea

Ingredients

500 grams of beef
500 grams of tomato sauce
1 onion
2 cloves of garlic
3 tablespoons of berbere
1 glass of water
Salt (to your liking)

Preparation (for 4 people)

Start by sautéing a finely minced onion in a non-stick saucepan. After five minutes, add three tablespoons of berbere, a glass of water and salt. On low heat, let the water evaporate, then add 500 grams of tomato sauce and if necessary, another glass of water. Let it boil for about fifteen minutes. Add 500 grams of cubed beef and two cloves of garlic and allow everything to simmer for about an hour or until the meat is fully cooked and the water has fully evaporated. Zighinì is usually served along with boiled eggs and steamed vegetables on injera bread. With your fingers, take a small piece of bread and pick up a morsel of meat and veggies.

Injera Bread

Ingredients

Semolina flour
Warm water

Preparation (for 8-12 people)

Mix two glasses of water with 150 grams of semolina flour in a large bowl (traditionally we use teff, a specific flour from Africa that is hard to find in the West). Once you have reached a homogeneous and liquid batter, cover the bowl and let the batter ferment at room temperature for three days. After the fermentation, heat up a non-stick pan and place a ladle full of batter into the pan. Let it cook for about two or three minutes on one side only. When ready, in order to make sure it doesn't dry up, keep the injera bread in a tight Tupperware container until ready to eat.

I learned how to cook at fifteen. My mother taught me how to make zighinì when we were in Sudan. The first time I prepared it in Italy, it did not come out well because I was not able to find the right flour. Also in Italy, the injera has to ferment for more than three days because the climate is much colder than Eritrea and Sudan. The most important ingredient for the preparation of zighinì is berbere, which is made of hot pepper and spices to season the meat.

Zighinì is prepared on special occasions, such as weddings or religious festivities. In Eritrea, we serve homemade alcoholic beverages like mes and suwa for celebratory meals. During a wedding or for the birth of a child, we throw confetti, just like in Italy. But when I got married, I unfortunately could not celebrate as I would have liked, not sharing these offerings with everyone. But it's a long story.

I was born in a refugee camp in Sudan because my parents escaped from Eritrea. In 2003, when I was fifteen, after being told that the situation in Eritrea had improved, my family decided to move back. That was the first time I met my country of origin. When we arrived, we discovered a situation far from peaceful. My brothers and I spoke Arabic and did not speak Tigrinya, so in school, we were placed in classes with children four years younger than us.

In 2006, a military squad arrived at our school and took my brothers away for military service. They were taken to a training camp, a horrible place where both women and men serve mandatory military service. Rape and torture takes place in these camps, and often those who get to return home never recover and suffer from mental illnesses. One of my brothers came back from the camp and told us terrible and absurd stories. My other brother died there, we found out from a phone call. My mother couldn't even see his body. She was distraught by the pain.

After the death of my brother, my father went from office to office denouncing the atrocious life of Eritrean people, shouting his sorrow for their condition and their land, and in the end he was also imprisoned. To this day I don't know if he is dead or alive.

In Eritrea, you cannot have your own life. It is decided for you. For a long time, I used go out very little because you can be kidnapped and taken to a training camp. My boyfriend and I decided to accelerate our wedding and to postpone the celebration to avoid being enlisted in the military.

My husband worked for the government. He used to do odd jobs—masonry, fixing roads, cleaning. Everyone in Eritrea has to serve the government in this way in exchange for five euros per month. After the wedding, though, my husband decided to stop. They came looking for him at home and he was forced to flee.

When they returned for him again, I was two months pregnant with my first child and I simply declared I did not know where he was. I was taken by force and locked up at Adabeto prison, where I stayed for two months. One day, I was beaten so much that I fell and lost consciousness. They took me to a hospital. Fortunately, I did not suffer any complications with my pregnancy. After that incident, I was released and returned to my parents' home. My father had been taken to Adabeto too. By then, I lost all traces of my husband. I used to talk about him to my son, I showed him his pictures. He knew his father only through photographs. Life in Eritrea was not peaceful, it was impossible. That is why I escaped with my son and my mother to try and return to Sudan.

But even there, life for Christians is difficult and I had to be careful. I could not go out, I had to cover myself. Life was hell. Luckily, in Sudan, I reunited with my husband, and my son met his father for the first time. We decided to leave Africa because we understood that our lives were at risk. Now we continued our journey.

Standing with two hundred women, men and children, we went across the desert in a pickup truck. We were sick, close to dying, but we were able to reach Libya. When we arrived in Tripoli, my second child was born. He was only five months old when we went across the Mediterranean Sea for eight days, along with 270 people.

We arrived in Lampedusa two weeks before the October 3, 2013 shipwreck in which so many people like us, and children as small as ours, lost their lives. Our boat was also about to sink but we were lucky that help arrived in time. I have a beautiful memory of our arrival on the island: generous people, kind rescuers. But it was all very brief.

During our time at the center where we stayed, no one wanted to be identified. They were eager to continue their journey and ask for asylum elsewhere. After three days, we were taken to Camp Pozzallo. The place was horrible. It was not a camp but a huge tent where two hundred people slept together on the floor, and bathrooms and showers were shared by men and women. There was daily fighting with the police because no one wanted to be fingerprinted and be profiled, but they forced all of us to go through the process.

After two days without any information, they ordered us to board a bus. We kept asking where we were going, and they kept claiming not to know. My husband, my mother, my two children and I were already sitting when the doors of the bus were suddenly reopened and we were told to get off. Everyone was confused. We all exited the bus and some people started to run away. Others were angry and screaming. I saw the police grab those who were running, and in the confusion, I lost sight of my husband. We were ordered again to enter the bus and the doors were closed. The bus left among the confusion and my husband was no longer by my side. We haven't seen him since that day.

My life now is in the hands of the commission that decides who can remain in Italy and who must go back to the hell from which they left.

When I prepare zighinì, I relive many pleasant and painful memories. All the familiar smells, the faces of loved ones. I think of my brother who is no longer with us, my father whose fate I don't know, my sister who lives in Canada and my husband whose whereabouts are still unknown to us.

Translated by Veruska Cantelli.
From: *Cum-panis: Storie di fuga, identità e memorie,
in quattro ricette* a cura di Associazione Culturale
Multietnica "La Kasbah Onlus," di Enza Papa e
Francesco Mollo Edizioni Erranti, 2014.

When the sea is rendered as slavery, violence and mourning are symbolized by spatial stasis. Aquatic stasis reflects temporal depth and death; in fact, water is an element "which remembers the dead"

"Heavy Waters: Waste and Atlantic Modernity," Elizabeth Deloughrey

The Mediterranean Abyss

Léopold Lambert

"What comes back from the abyss? It is a rumor of several centuries. And, it is the song of the Ocean's plains. Sonic shells rub themselves against skulls, bones and cannonball now turned green in the bottom of the Atlantic Ocean. In this abyss, there are cemeteries of the slave ships. Rapacities, violated borders, banners fell and picked up from the Western world. And who constellates the thick mat of the sons of Africa from whom a commerce emerged, those are out of nomenclature, no one knows their amount."

Édouard Glissant and Patrick Chamoiseau,
L'intraitable beauté du monde

What Caribbean philosophers and poets Édouard Glissant and Patrick Chamoiseau name "the abyss" (*le gouffre*) is the belly of the Atlantic Ocean, which swallowed two million African bodies during three centuries of the slave trade. Whether dead from the unfathomably atrocious conditions of life on the slave ship,[1] or thrown alive and unchained to the sea in case of contagious disease, rebellion, or of a chase by another ship, these millions of bodies that never reached the Americas' coasts populate a cemetery at the bottom of the ocean.

Another tragic cemetery now lies in the middle of the Mediterranean Sea. However, the oceanic abyss is different from the continental one. Once again, we turn to Édouard Glissant to think of the Mediterranean Sea as "a sea that concentrates,"[2] a sea around which empires have been built, transforming the tectonic fault into an imperial pond. Today, the sea continues to host a militarized territory: the Cyprus conflict, the war led by NATO along the Libyan coasts, and the Israeli blockade of Gaza are only the most spectacular examples of this militarization.

The sea also constitutes the hyper surveyed no-man's land of the Southern border of Fortress Europe.

After more than a century of colonial hegemony whose imperial violence established an indelible relation between both "sides" of the sea, Europe refused such a tie and found an ideal form of continental wall with the Mediterranean abyss. What constitutes a territory easy to monitor from the Northern coasts' point of view represents, on the contrary, a frightening last obstacle to cross after a dreadful journey for thousands of African migrants who can only turn to the clandestine and abusive channels of immigration, the official ones being closed by the administrative wall. The indifference with which we, Europeans, look at overpopulated, dilapidated boats sinking not far from our coasts is symptomatic of our impossible empathy for the otherness.[3]

Following the *Intermundia* research, we can say that the Mediterranean Abyss does not stand only for the cemetery of African bodies, but also for the transformational process that each migrant body undergoes through its crossing. When touching the European land, this body becomes an administrative, rightless subject that can be legally detained for an undetermined duration. As Stjepan Žgela and Ana Dana Beroš show us in the following pages, the architecture of migrant detention centers embodies the sordid means of detention of these rightless subjects.[4] Europe is populated by these particular prisons, which circumscribe a territory of exclusion within its own borders.

Lampedusa could be the antinomy of the abyss. Etymologically, it signifies a rock, emerging from the sea, an oasis in an aquatic desert, a haven located between Europe and Africa. The militarized history of Europe proves otherwise: in 1872, the eleven-year-old Kingdom of Italy established a penitentiary colony on the island. During the Second World War, it hosted a military base bombed by the allies and, in the 1970s–1980s, the Western part of the island was used for a NATO transmitter station. Today, the island is part of the enforcement of policies that recognize no rights to so-called "clandestine migrants." Lampedusa thus embodies only the rigid and defensive characteristics of the rock, regardless of its potential haven properties. In this regard, it fully contributes to the Mediterranean Abyss for which Europe is responsible.

Let's consider the map "Mediterranean Without Borders," an artwork by Sabine Réthoré (2013). It consists of a map of the Mediterranean Sea and its coastal regions that is subjected to two simple operations: a 90-degree tilt that places the North on the right side of the document, and a withdrawal of all lines usually signifying national borders. As such, the map appears to us as simultaneously familiar and peculiar. Through it, we recognize a space we know well, but our perception of it evolves thanks to the way it is represented. "Mediterranean Without Borders" represents territories that seem optically

closer to each other than when considered on a geopolitical map. The sea almost appears as a calm lake, where people on one bank would not feel essentially different from their neighbors on the opposite one. We can no longer see three continents struggling to exist but, rather, the sea as gathering lands around it. The names of the cities are worth reading out loud. Their sounds reveal more regional identities blending into each other, than strictly differentiated national belongings.

This map is our manifesto against the Abyss: it changes our imaginary and recounts the Mediterranean's profound relation that exists between the bodies living along its coasts. We should not misunderstand the nature of this relation as Édouard Glissant defined it. It is not a candid wish for friendly rapports but, rather, the indelible mark of a common imaginary (including its past and current violence) shared by the nations involved. The Abyss and its imperial violence will not be forgotten, but a *creolity* (*créolité*) can emerge beyond it if we are ready to embrace the relation and its hybridation of identities.

1   C.L.R. James, *The Black Jacobins: Toussaint L'Ouverture and the San Domingo Revolution* (Random House, 1989), and Édouard Glissant, *Poetics of the Relation*, trans. Betsy Wing, Ann Arbor: University of Michigan Press, 1997.
2   Édouard Glissant, *Poetics of the Relation*, trans. Betsy Wing, Ann Arbor: University of Michigan Press, 1997.
3   In addition to the work presented in this exhibition, we can refer to the chapter "The Left to Die Boat," in Forensic Architecture, *Forensis: The Architecture of Public Truth*, Berlin: Sternberg, 2014.
4   See also Tings Chak, *Undocumented: The Architecture of Migrant Detention Centers*, Westmount QC: The Architecture Observer, 2014.

"The Mediterranean Abyss," foreword to Intermundia exhibition catalog (2014). Exibition curated by Ana Dana Beroš and presented at the section "Monditalia" at the 2014 Venice Biennale.

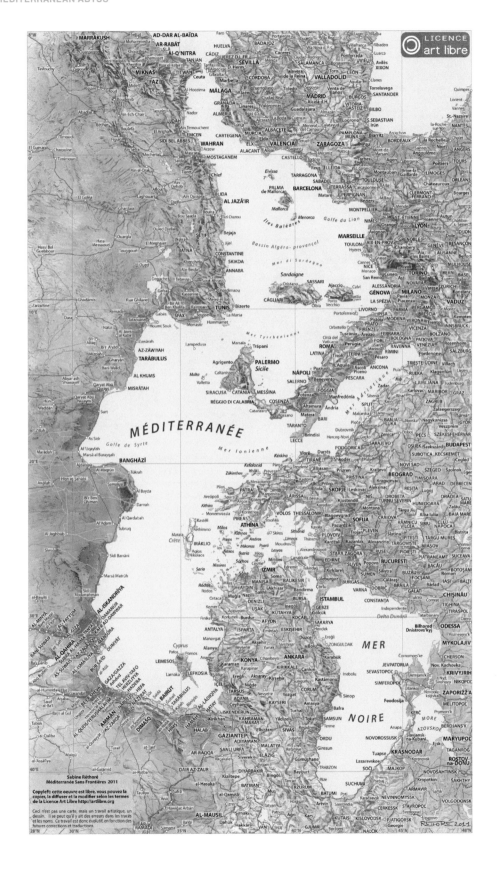

Cimitero delle Barche. The boats that capsized bringing the refugees, dumped
across the road from the port that Lampedusans call "The Boat Cemetery."
Documentation photos by Stjepan Žgela and Ana Dana Beroš; field recording for
Intermundia sound installation by Ana Dana Beroš.

CIE di Contrada Imbriacola. Vacant Identification and Expulsion Centre for immigrants in Lampedusa, temporarily closed due to reconstruction and erection of two new pavilions in April 2014. Documentation photos by Stjepan Žgela and Ana Dana Beroš.

Interior of the installation. Photo by Ana Dana Beroš.

Intermundia as a part of the "Monditalia" exhibition, of the 14th Venice biennale of Architecture, 2014. Photo by Ana Dana Beroš.

EARTH PARADISE. Embarkment point for immigrants. Named the most beautiful beach in the world. From documentary film *Hotel Europa*, by Ivana Dragičević and Dinko Cepak, photo by Dinko Cepak, 2013, Lampedusa, Italy.

HERE AND THERE. The portrait of a young man called Prince Wale Shonyiki, the asylee who left his native Nigeria due to a family tragedy caused by religious and ethnic conflicts. The photo shows Prince during his leisure time recorded in the river of Mrežnica, in the vicinity of Zagreb. Photo by Ana Mihalić, 2013, Zagreb.

A Manual For Living

Chika Unigwe

"This is how you roll a condom on." The instructor tears open a packet and without taking her eyes off us, begins to sheath the plastic penis on the table. I can hear Honey snickering beside me. The rest of us are trying hard not to laugh. The plastic penis is pale yellow. Oyibo penis, Honey whispers and giggles some more. Honey is fifteen. It is no wonder this amuses her. The instructor ignores her. "You," she points at me. "Come and try." She throws me a condom.

In a few days, we will leave. Honey and Jojo and I are going to Italy. Mary and Juliet are destined for Belgium. Pat and two women who arrived only two days ago are the German crew. We have been here already, cooped up in the house in Lagos for almost ten days. Freedom is near! Freedom and money, Honey shouts later in our room that night. She starts singing P-Square's "Chop My Money!"

Honey, Pat and I share a room but we don't know each other's real names but that doesn't prevent us from being a family. Madam Koko, who runs this house with an iron fist, warns every new comer, "We don't want to know who you were before coming here. Your past is of no interest to us, but on the crossing, you'll have no one else but each other." We use our new names so that we can get used to them before we arrive in Europe and begin our new lives working in the red light district. We are given language lessons (just the basics); we are taught to pirouette for customers. We are given the skills to survive.

Three days after our condom lesson we begin our journey, first by bus to Ghana.

I call my mother from Ghana. I am doing this for her, too. A widow with five children and a pension she cannot rely on. Very soon, she complained one night, she would not even be able to buy kerosene for the lanterns.

We go by truck from Ghana to Niger. Agadev is dust and thirst. Days of waiting in the desert for the carriage to Libya. Water is rationed and anyone who complains is asked to drink their urine. At first, we shudder and laugh, Honey most of all. But it does not take long before we are actually holding our noses and drinking our own pee.

Next stop Libya. In Sabha, I sleep with a man whose name I do not know for bathing soap and water. I cannot turn back even if I wanted to. And why should I, having come this far?

One morning, before dawn we are packed like sardines in a wooden boat. Two, three days. You'll be in Italy, our contact tells us. I close my eyes so I do not see the sea. Honey laughs and says, It's calm, Evbu. See?

This is how you die. The calm sea lulls you to sleep. The boat begins to leak. Water wakes you up. Honey's screams pierce through your ears as the boat begins to sink.

The sea will take what it will.

De Koepel prison in Arnhem is one of three Panopticon-style detention facilities in the Netherlands. Designed by Johan Frederik Metzelaar, the prison was completed in 1886. Photo by Mujtaba Jalali.

Refugees languish in the imposing De Koepel prison in Arnhem, Netherlands.
Photo by Mujtaba Jalali.

Criminalizing Food

Veruska Cantelli interviews Mary Bosworth

The conviviality of weaving stories while folding bread, stirring while entering the angles of the self, tracing the urgency of familiar smells. These are some ways in which food shapes our lives. But in the context of dislocation and detention, food enters back into the realm of the politics of sustenance. When food is denied, controlled, rationed, part of one's life management becomes someone else's domain, and the act of giving swiftly starts to accommodate discipline. Images of food lines in refugee camps in Europe, the banning of meals as a tactic for keeping migrants from settling—which led to the arrest of volunteers in the Italian town of Ventimiglia—are just two examples in which food in the current European migrant crisis is being turned into a weapon of control.

Overabundance is countered by an image of scarcity: the amount of a scoop or the frugality of a lunch consumed from a plastic plate serve to manipulate belief in deficit, overpopulation, the impossibility of aiding "excessive numbers of migrants." The video from a reception center in Hungary showing police deliberately throwing sandwiches at refugees clearly illustrates the extent to which desperation is exploited for amusement. We don't have to go far to connect these events with the dehumanizing practices concocted by histories of colonization: "Animalization forms part of a larger, more diffuse mechanism of naturalization: the reduction of the cultural to the biological, the tendency to associate the colonized with the vegetative and the instinctual rather than the learned and the cultural," writes Mary Bosworth. Handling and regulating food is another way in which crowds can be dominated, restrained, branded.

In our conversation, Bosworth, author of *Inside Immigration Detention,* a meticulous and humane study of the everyday life of migrants in British detention centers underscores that "[t]he politics of food in detention revolve around the issue of choice and culture. Those who observe particular diets, e.g. Halal, vegan or vegetarian, are very suspicious about the claims of the institution that the food is appropriate. They do not like being forced to eat at particular times." The control exercised through food is manifested in scheduling, issues of choice, quality, and restrictions, but also in the exclusion from its preparation.

Bosworth points out that the micromanaging of meals goes as far as prohibiting fresh produce in the rooms, essentially driving detainees to live off packaged food that can be made in the microwave or with a kettle. Conviviality in these circumstances is not the spontaneous, deliberate instance of bonding, but a practice artificially managed by staff. While almost all the women's centers in the United Kingdom, Bosworth adds, now have cultural kitchenettes, a space that a group of people can book to prepare food and eat it together, "in the men's institutions, the centers are run a little differently. In Colnbrook, for instance, one man usually works alone, with some officers monitoring him, to cook for a small group of friends who are then allowed to enter and eat together. In each center, staff is concerned about access to knives and sharp objects." The continuous pairing of migration with criminality finds its place in detention centers, where people seeking relocation from war-torn countries are quickly turned into potential violent individuals.

Sharing a meal is, like in any situation of surveillance, an affair that often does not include the workers. Detainees and those who supervise them remain segregated, and this separation is reflected even among migrants. "Socially, food plays an ambiguous role in the centers," says Bosworth. In some institutions, like the Campsfield House, outside Oxford, and Tinsley House, near Gatwick airport, detainees and staff eat together in a dining hall. When I have been there, I have noticed that the men organize themselves, with distinct nationality groups usually eating together, and the staff sitting separately. In other facilities, like Colnbrook, the men are served their food in the housing units. They either eat in tables in the center of the space, or take their plates of food back to their rooms."

In the limbo of detention centers, migrants' physical and psychological conditions often get worse, not only because of precarious conditions, but also because of the poor quality of what they eat. "As people's health deteriorates in detention, they often long for fresh fruit and vegetables, and for home cooking and conviviality." Her extensive work has put her in touch with many stories of escape and she emphasizes that food and cuisine "are topics that often come up in interviews. Men and women miss their local dishes. They often describe particular recipes they used to make and the diverse ingredients that exist in their countries. Even those who do not want to return to the places where they were born may be nostalgic for those tastes."

The recipes included here are journeys into memory, into the fear of its disappearance. The stories that accompany them reaffirm the most fundamental of human needs: not food itself, but the community that it allows to form and define. Identity is inaugurated through the offering of a laborious meal. Denying this practice means to sever a bond, a sense of recognition with that filament one calls home.

Dearden, Lizzie. "British man among aid volunteers arrested for giving food to refugees stranded in Italy." *Independent*, March 24, 2017, http://www.independent.co.uk/news/world/europe/british-man-refugee-volunteer-food-arrest-ventimiglia-italy-gerard-bonnet-roya-citoyenne-group-a7648661.html

Dinham, Paddy. "Food Queue with Echoes of Europe's Dark Past: Freezing Migrants Wait for Aid in Belgrade Today in Pictures Chillingly Similar to Those from the Second World War." *Mailonline*, January 10, 2017, http://www.dailymail.co.uk/news/article-4107102/Belgrade-migrants-wait-food-pictures-similar-Second-World-War.html

Gentleman, Amelia. "Calais Mayor Bans Distribution of Food to Migrants." *Guardian*, March 2, 2017, https://www.theguardian.com/world/2017/mar/02/calais-mayor-bans-distribution-of-food-to-migrants

Shohat, Ella and Stam, Robert. *Unthinking Eurocentrism: Multiculturalism and the Media.* Routledge, 2013.

Walker, Peter. "Refugees Forced to Scramble for Food by Police in Hungary." *Guardian*, September 11, 2015, https://www.theguardian.com/world/2015/sep/11/refugees-roszke-hungary-police-food-camp

Interview with Mary Bosworth was conducted via email.

So memorize this night of hurt by heart. You may well be the narrator, the narrative, and the narrated. Do not forget this narrow winding road that carries you, and that you carry, toward the boisterous unknown, that will cast doubts upon you and your people.

You ask: What is the meaning of "refugee"?

They will say: One who is uprooted from his homeland.

"In the Presence of Absence,"
Mahmoud Darwish

Maps of Exile

Hassan Ghedi Santur

"We can't stop. We're not rocks—progress, migration, motion is . . .
modernity. . . It's what living things do. We desire. . . Even if we go
faster than we should. We can't wait. And wait for what?"

Tony Kushner, *Angels in America*

Tents in flames. Billowing smoke. Broken bed frames and abandoned plastic chairs. In a hotel room in Mogadishu, Somalia, some seven thousand miles away, I watch the Calais Jungle burn. I stare at the apocalyptic scenes from Calais on the television news, unable to turn away. Among the countless brown and black faces wrapped in blankets, waiting for buses that would evacuate them from the infamous migrant camp, I search for a familiar face. In the distance, I see the Church of Angel Michael. Its large cross defiantly stands above the carnage all around it. It is an Ethiopian Orthodox Church made of cardboard, plastic sheets, and a corrugated tin roof held together with a few pieces of wood. It was in that church that I interviewed Solomon Getchawu, who had lived in the Jungle for over a year. He and his friends from Ethiopia built the church with their own hands from discarded material they gathered.

The erasure of the Jungle started on October 25, 2016. In just three days, the camp that had existed since the mid-1990s, and which, over the years, became one of the largest illegal settlements in Western Europe, was declared no more. "This is the end of the 'Jungle,'" Calais regional prefect Fabienne Buccio told Reuters. "Mission accomplished,"[1] he said.

The Jungle's destruction had been long in the making. Since the Paris terror attacks in November 2015, the French government had signaled its desire to shut the camp down. In September 2016, French President Francois Hollande visited Calais, a port town in the country's north, and promised residents of the town that his government would "definitively, entirely and rapidly" close the camp.

It was not the first time that an unpopular president facing re-election vowed to get tough on immigrants and close the camp. Several presidents have come and gone, but the camp survived their promises to destroy it. This time was different. By October 28, more than six thousand of the camp's estimated nine thousand residents had been moved to hundreds of reception centers scattered across France, even as demonstrations broke out in several towns with residents taking to the streets shouting, "We Don't Want Them!"[2]

For many of the refugees and migrants, this is the end of a long, nightmarish journey. Out of anger, desperation, or perhaps revenge, some of the residents set fire to the very homes they built for themselves in the sprawling camp. Forced to relocate to cities and towns across the country, they must resign themselves to the very thing they never wanted to do in the first place: seek asylum in France. For a variety of reasons, the United Kingdom, which lies just on the other side of the Straight of Dover, was their promised land, never France.

For others, however, the fight to stay continues. About three thousand migrants refused to participate in the government's relocation plan. Many fled to nearby forests where they planned to wait out the operation; some headed for a nearby refugee camp in Dunkirk; others "sleep in ditches near the coast, (then) continue (on towards)"[3] Great Britain. Some have also vowed to rebuild the Jungle elsewhere in Calais, while many others have headed for the capital. Since the Jungle's demolition in late October, there has been a steady rise in the number of make-shift camps going up in parts of Paris, such as the neighborhood of Saint-Denis. According to estimates by local NGOs, "some 2,000–2,500 migrants are sleeping outside Stalingrad Metro station."[4]

Among the countless African faces I see on the television screen, I seek out Ahmed Ibrahim Sa'eed's. I spent five days with him in the Calais Jungle in the final days of 2015. He shared with me his remarkable journey from Somalia to Northern France. Like tens of thousands of African economic migrants, Ahmed risked his life in search of a dream. His hopes were fueled by an unshakable belief that he was meant for more than his homeland could offer him. He was among the lucky. Too many of his fellow Africans paid for their ambition with their lives. In November 2015, Ahmed made it safely to the Calais Jungle. His arrival, though, marked only the beginning of a great struggle.

Just as the Mediterranean Sea has come to symbolize the extraordinary lengths to which the world's dispossessed are willing to go to set foot on European soil, the Calais Jungle had become a symbol of sorts. The camp represented a cautionary political tale for some and a moral outrage for others. For Europeans opposed to liberal migration regimes, the Jungle represented

the continent's failure to protect its borders and keep the "unwanted" at bay. For many others, it represented Europe's inability to deal with the ongoing migration crisis ethically or humanely. But the Jungle was more than any of this. It was a physical reality; a place on Europe's map; a place of refuge for the world's exiles. Up until its recent destruction by the French government, the camp was a place built by migrants, for migrants. For all its squalor and depravation, it was home to thousands of disparate, desperate people. It was their unequivocal choice against the stagnation and impotency that characterizes most reception centers in Europe. In those places, refugees are often treated less like people and more like undesirable goods in a warehouse.

————

"Traffic! Traffic!" Ahmed Ibrahim Sa'eed hears someone yell in Arabic, jolting him from the depths of sleep. It is early morning. He sits up and looks around, disoriented. His eyes focus on the person yelling "traffic." It is his friend from Sudan standing by the door of the tent trying to wake everyone up. The opportunity they had been waiting for has at last presented itself.

Ahmed is one of the first to run out. He dresses in such a hurry that his shoelaces are still undone as he stumbles into the cold morning air. He is shocked to see so many camp residents pouring from their tents and into the alleyways leading to the highway. He does not know exactly what the cause of the traffic is, but judging from the mass exodus he is witnessing, Ahmed figures it is a bad accident that has brought the traffic on the highway to an absolute standstill. As he and hundreds of other camp residents run along the muddy, unpaved roads past the overhead bridge, the unofficial gate of the camp, all he can think is: "This could be it." November 25, 2015, could be the day he finally manages to sneak into the back of a cargo truck bound for England. Every decision he has made since August 2015, when he first set foot in Italy— every bus and train ride he's taken from Italy to Austria and Germany to France has been leading to the day he would be safely carried across the Strait of Dover and into England.

It seems to Ahmed that half the camp's population is running along with him. He looks around and notices that everyone, like himself, is only half-dressed. The usual scarfs, hats and gloves have all been abandoned for fear of missing an epic traffic jam when the nearby highway would be clogged with idling trucks, waiting like a gift from God. There is an unspoken tradition in the camp that when someone finds out about a traffic jam, they call or text their friends and fellow camp residents, urging them to drop everything. People lining up for breakfast abandon their queues to join the exodus. People brushing their teeth at the communal taps make a run for the highway.

When Ahmed finally gets to the highway, the traffic is as "good" as he had hoped. Trucks line the expressway as far as the eye can see. He and his friends scatter, hoping to find the perfect hiding place deep among the cargo in the back of the trucks. When confronted with so many migrants on the highway, truck drivers never try to stop them from boarding. They simply lock their doors and wait for the police to arrive. In the meantime, camp residents frantically maneuver between trucks, opening the back doors of every one, desperate to find an ideal place to stow away.

Ahmed tries the doors of several trucks. They are all jammed shut. He is getting more desperate by the second. It is just a matter of time before the dreaded Compagnies Républicaines de Sécurité (CRS Police) show up with their metal batons, pepper spray, and tear gas canisters. At last, he finds a rear door that is open, but he is met with a chorus of voices yelling at him to find another truck to hide in. He makes a quick decision to leave the pack and find other trucks in the back of the line that have not been claimed. He runs past forty or so trucks, trying his best to avoid eye contact with the drivers glaring down at him. Finally, the rear door of a semi-trailer opens. Unlike some of the other trucks, it has plenty of room for hiding. It is transporting large aluminum cylinders about waist high that are placed vertically in rows. "The perfect hiding place," Ahmed thinks. As he climbs inside one of the tubes, he hears the door open. He watches impatiently as four men and a woman climb up. Part of him resents them for invading his hiding place. The more generous part of him wants for them what he wants for himself, so he tells them to get in quickly and hide in the other cylinders.

Crouched down inside the tubes so that their heads will not be seen, they sit in the dark, waiting for a long time for the truck to move. The vehicle finally comes to life and starts to move, slowly at first, then gathering speed. This is the moment Ahmed has been waiting for since he came to Calais in early November. He has made over twenty attempts. This time will be different. Ahmed feels as though Allah has finally answered his prayers.

After a few minutes of slow, steady driving, the truck stops. Ahmed hears distant voices. Suddenly the door swings open. He peeks his head up to see what is happening. It is another one of the camp boys. Relief washes over him. He motions for him to shut the door quickly and find a place to hide. Ahmed and the others sit in their individual tubes, waiting, praying for the truck to move again. Shortly after, the door swings open again. Standing at the door of the truck are four CRS police in their navy-blue uniforms, complete with shoulder and knee pads, black helmets and clubs. They look as though they are on the frontlines of a war. Two of them climb up while the other two stand on the street by the door. One of them starts yelling: "Allez! Allez!" Ahmed and the others are trapped; their great escape is over before it even begins.

Ahmed watches one of the officers walk toward him, baton in hand. He stands up and gets out of his hiding place, hands raised in the air. "Don't hit. Don't hit," he yells. As soon as he says the words, he realizes he is in deep trouble. Hidden from the scrutiny of the press and the civilian world, the CRS police have developed a fearsome reputation for doing to camp residents whatever they please with impunity. Ahmed tries to get out of the truck, but sees a baton coming at him. Miraculously, he manages to duck out of its way. The officer raises his club again, this time directly at Ahmed's face. Instinctively, he raises his hand to shield his face and head and feels the baton land on his wrist. Unbearable pain shoots through his entire body and he screams in agony. He hears the cries from the woman who is hiding in the truck with him, but he cannot not see what is being done to her; it is dim and he is dizzy with pain.

Cradling his wrist, Ahmed finally manages to stumble onto the tarmac of the highway. As he tries to run away, he looks back and sees the woman fall from the truck. She tries to get up and run but she cannot stand up. Two of the men traveling with her grab a shoulder each and carry her away. Fleeing the scene, Ahmed can still hear from the inside of the truck the screams of one of the men who had not managed to extricate himself as quickly as he did. Ahmed scurries into the nearby bushes along the highway, desperate to get back to the safety of the camp.

———————

I have spent much of the day walking around the Jungle. It is home to about nine thousand refugees and migrants, most of them from Africa, the Middle East, and some as far away as

Iran and Afghanistan. Ahmed has graciously agreed to give me a tour. We walk around, trying our best not to fall in the slippery, muddy alleyways as we survey the many tents that comprise the Jungle. Ahmed is still wearing a cast from his run in with the CRS police four weeks ago.

It has been raining for several days and the alleyways and unpaved roads connecting the camp's various neighborhoods are rivers of gray mud. The constant winds blowing from the Strait of Dover have been making things even worse. The most ubiquitous sound in the camp is that of plastic sheeting snapping in the wind—a grating, never-ending soundtrack. Despite the horrendous living conditions, everywhere I look, I see evidence of human ingenuity. Small shops line the roads of the camp selling soft drinks, chips, toothpaste, shampoo, soap and just about anything else you can imagine. There are also some eateries where one can find authentic Afghan dishes: lamb kebab, saffron rice and oven-made naan, diced chicken and baked potatoes. These shops are owned by well-to-do people who live outside the camp but sell goods inside it for profit. Serious money is being made here. There are also a few large tea houses where residents spend their evenings huddled together socializing and watching European football matches over tea and hookah. For a few hours in the evenings, before heading back to their cold, crowded sleeping tents, these well-heated tea houses provide the residents a chance not only to connect with each other but with the lives they left behind.

While walking around the camp with Ahmed, his easy rapport with almost everyone we come across strikes me. With his quiet intellect and graciousness, the extensive network of friendships Ahmed has cultivated in his few months living in the camp is remarkable. Everywhere he takes me, someone gives him a warm hug and speaks to him in Arabic, Somali or English. Perhaps these are the human skills one must perfect when one has spent almost his entire life as a refugee. In many ways, Ahmed's migration to Europe began twenty-four years earlier, when he was only two years old.

————

In 1992, life in Mogadishu, the capital city of Somalia, was hell on earth. Only the year before, in January 1991, the government of dictator Mohamed Siad Barre, who ruled Somalia for twenty-two years, fell following a bloody uprising of clan-led opposition groups. By the time U.S. Marines stormed the beaches of Mogadishu in 1993, fighting had killed fifty thousand Somalis, and an estimated three hundred thousand more died from starvation due to famine. It was in this environment of clan violence, lawlessness and famine in Southern Somalia that Ahmed's family fled the capital. Ahmed was only two years old at the time. His family was among the hundreds of thousands of Somalis who fled to neighboring countries.

Ahmed's parents decided to try their luck in Ethiopia. When life became too difficult there, the family headed for Djibouti, a poor, tiny country by the Red Sea where they lived until 1997. Then, once again, they relocated to Hargeisa, capital city of the self-declared independent state of Somaliland. Amid all this moving from place to place, Ahmed's parents still managed to send him to primary school. Once settled in Hargeisa, Ahmed continued his education and finished secondary school. He had always loved studying and wanted to continue his education. Figuring out a way to do so became the next great challenge of his life.

In 1991, Somaliland officially seceded from the rest of Somalia. In the following years, while other parts of the country were mired in civil war, Somaliland established a somewhat functioning government, reopened schools, and set conditions for life to gradually return to normal.

Still, the newly established country remained one of the poorest in the world. With no economy to speak of in the capital and competition for seats at the few functioning universities in the region fierce, Ahmed decided that staying in Hargeisa, as many of his cohorts had done, was out of the question. There were no jobs for a recent high school graduate like himself. He was certain he did not want to spend his days hanging out at local tea shops playing cards with his friends and fantasizing about an alternate life. He was far too ambitious to resign himself to the meager realities around him. Ahmed made up his mind to leave. He told me that this decision was among the hardest things he had ever done. Saying goodbye to his parents and nine siblings was very painful. Twenty years old, Ahmed left Hargeisa, his family, and relative stability for an uncertain future in Sudan.

Leaving Hargeisa for Sudan was the first act of migration that Ahmed had made alone. After receiving his parents' blessing in the fall of 2010, Ahmed got on a bus, travelled all the way through Ethiopia and finally ended up in Khartoum, capital city of Sudan. For a while, he was not sure if he would remain in Sudan, but was persuaded by friends in Khartoum to give it more time and look around for an inexpensive university where he could continue his education. Shortly after, he started at a local college, studying computer networking and working odd jobs to pay his school fees. Ahmed told me he loved studying at the university. Circumstances may have been difficult, and whatever money he made from his various odd jobs went straight toward his tuition, but he had a mission. He felt he was making progress. He was always happiest when he was working toward concrete, attainable goals.

However, in four years, that feeling Ahmed dreaded most—the feeling of stagnation— crept up again as he graduated university with a bachelor's degree but little else to show for his efforts. Sudan is not the kind of country where a recent university graduate, no matter how smart or qualified, can expect to land a professional job. The generally high unemployment rate in the country was far worse for a young Somali immigrant with no connections to the elites of Sudanese society, where access to jobs tended to be concentrated.

From the time of his graduation in 2014 until 2015, when he finally left Sudan, Ahmed tried many times to immigrate to other parts of the world legally. For instance, he wanted to continue his studies and complete a master's degree, so he applied for various scholarships at universities in Germany and Romania, with no luck. He also tried to travel legally to Cairo, where he had several friends, but the Egyptian embassy in Khartoum rejected his visa application. With his attempts to migrate legally frustrated at every turn, Ahmed made the decision to do what countless other young African men have done before him: he decided to go to Europe by any means possible. He called his friends in Cairo, who told him what routes to take and how much money he would need for the journey. His mind was made up. There was no turning back.

In June 2016, Ahmed embarked on a journey across continents. He knew full well the dangers, and he also knew that, were he to tell his parents of his decision, they would do their utmost to dissuade him. Ahmed knew that the journey he was about to take could end in death, but he did not want any doubts planted in his head, especially by loved ones. So, he kept his parents in the dark about his trip. Since Sudan and Egypt share a long, porous border, Ahmed went to a tiny border town in Northern Sudan (he could not remember its name) where he paid a Sudanese guard to sneak him into Egypt illegally. He stayed a day in the picturesque, ancient town of Aswan by the banks of the Nile along Egypt's southern frontier. From Aswan, he took a train to Cairo, where he stayed for three months with friends.

When he was ready for the next leg of his journey, Ahmed travelled north to the port city of Alexandria, situated along Egypt's Mediterranean coast. He stayed there with another friend from Sudan who put him in contact with a boat smuggler. Arranging the sea journey was a clandestine process full of secret meetings since the Egyptian government was clamping down on people smuggling. Ahmed paid $2,500 to a middleman in Alexandria who worked for the owner of a smuggling boat. On September 14, 2016, at midnight, he went to the rundown docks on the outskirts of the city, where three fishing boats were waiting in the dark. Ahmed was led aboard and they set sail.

At 2:00am, a few hours after leaving the coast of Alexandria, a large ship anchored in international waters met the three fishing boats. Such a large vessel would have been spotted by the Egyptian Maritime forces, so the smaller, less visible boats ferry the migrants to the large ship in the middle of the sea. Unlike many of the other migrants, who did not have life jackets, Ahmed paid his smuggler an extra seventy dollars for a used life jacket just in case the vessel encountered any troubles in the cold Mediterranean. He was ready to take risks, but preferred they be calculated ones rather than acts of blind faith.

The large ship in which Ahmed and his fellow travelers found themselves had three levels. Women and children were separated from the men in a different hull of the ship. All three levels were packed with migrants that Ahmed estimated to comprise close to four hundred people. The ship was so crowded that there was no room to stretch his legs, and when he went to use the toilet, he had to step over people sleeping on the floor. It is a scene eerily reminiscent of the Middle Passage, except no one was in chains and they all paid small fortunes to be there. The ship spent five days at sea, which was auspicious. The trip from Egypt to Italy can take upwards of ten days in bad weather, often resulting in sea-sickness, shortages of food, and dehydration for the passengers. Ahmed and the others were given food twice a day, which consisted of flat bread with jam and butter. They were also given large bottles of water, which four people had to share.

Early in the morning of September 19, the journey came to a safe end when a Norwegian rescue ship spotted their boat about two hours off the coast of Sicily. Life jackets were distributed to everyone on board, and the passengers were moved to the rescue ship, which took them to a port in southern Sicily. From there, they were moved to a large reception center where they were processed. Those needing medical attention were treated. They stayed at this reception center for three days and were given clean clothes, access to showers, three meals a day and beds to sleep on. For many, this was the first time they had slept on a bed in weeks.

Instead of going to Rome, as he had told the officers at the reception center, Ahmed boarded a bus to Bari, the coastal town on the Adriatic Sea where a friend lived. A quiet tourist town with lots of pretty attractions, Bari was a welcoming sight for someone who had crossed several African countries and the Mediterranean Sea. But Ahmed was on a mission to get to Calais, France. He had decided before leaving Cairo that the Calais Jungle, which he read about in the news, was his best chance at sneaking into England. So, after two weeks of much needed rest in his friend's small but nice apartment, he was ready to continue his march toward France. In Bari, Ahmed met an Ethiopian man who made his living transporting refugees and migrants across Europe. For an undocumented migrant like Ahmed, travelling in a private car would have been much safer since the chance of being stopped by police is next to nil. However, traveling in this fashion is not cheap.

The man told Ahmed that he could drive him from Bari all the way to Frankfurt, and even as

far as Stockholm, for five hundred euros. That was a price way beyond Ahmed's meager budget. Instead, Ahmed's friend bought him a bus ticket to Munich for only seventy euros. According to Ahmed, traveling across Europe by bus requires a great deal of research to learn which buses cross which borders and which borders are patrolled by guards. In preparation, Ahmed spent countless hours in cyber cafés studying Google Maps, familiarizing himself with various routes and borders, and mapping out the best path to the future he envisioned for himself. Having this information has become more crucial for migrants on the move. Since the Paris attacks of November 2015, several EU countries have suspended the Schengen Agreement that abolished internal border controls within Western Europe. This has made it exceedingly difficult for migrants to cross borders without being detected. In fact, once Ahmed crossed into Germany, the police stopped him in the town of Rosenheim, just southeast of Munich. He was detained and had his fingerprints taken, something he had managed to avoid ever since he landed in Italy. Once a migrant is fingerprinted, it goes into the EU database which makes it extremely difficult to apply for asylum elsewhere in the EU. Ahmed was transported, by German police, to the Bayernkaserne Refugee Centre.

Bayernkaserne, a former military barracks, was refurbished to accommodate the huge number of refugees pouring into Germany. Ahmed's heart sank when he saw the center, which he said looked like a jail. He thought he was actually being taken to prison. Once he saw the inside of the center, however, he was relieved. Despite being crowded with refugees and migrants from all over the world, Ahmed told me that Bayernkaserne was one of the cleanest, most well run centers he had seen, and far superior to the dirty, overcrowded reception centers in southern Italy. He stayed at the center for two weeks, long enough to plan his escape. As nice as the center was, Ahmed saw it as nothing more than an unplanned detour on his way to Calais.

The residents were free to leave the refugee center during the day but had to return before sunset. Ahmed, however, set off one morning for good. He made it to the Munich bus station and purchased a ticket for a Frankfurt-bound coach. After about a six-hour bus ride, Ahmed arrived. From Frankfurt, he bought another bus ticket, this time to Paris, for twenty-six euros. While waiting in the station for the night bus to Paris, Ahmed met three young Sudanese men. Since he spoke Arabic, he started chatting with them and discovered that, like him, they were also headed for Calais. Ahmed was elated to have some company to ease the nerve-wracking soli-tude of his travels. He and his three new friends arrived in Paris around 5:00am. They then waited until around 9:00am for the bus that

would take them on to Calais. While buying their tickets in Paris, they were approached by an Iraqi man who was distraught and on the verge of tears. He had heard them speaking Arabic and approached them, saying that after weeks of traveling to get to Paris, he had run out of money and only had seven euros left (the bus to Calais cost seventeen euros). Ahmed and the three others chipped in and paid the difference. They boarded a Euroline bus and headed north.

About eight hours later, just after sunset, Ahmed and the others arrived in Calais. None of them knew how to get to the Jungle. At the bus station, Ahmed looked around trying to pick out other migrants by the way they dressed or carried themselves. In halting English, he asked one for directions to the camp. The man

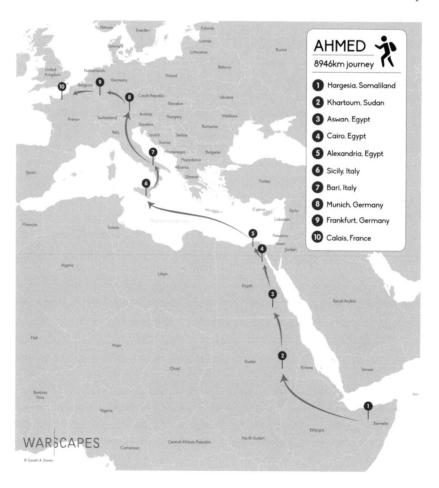

AHMED 🚶
8946km journey

1 Hargesia, Somaliland
2 Khartoum, Sudan
3 Aswan, Egypt
4 Cairo, Egypt
5 Alexandria, Egypt
6 Sicily, Italy
7 Bari, Italy
8 Munich, Germany
9 Frankfurt, Germany
10 Calais, France

WARSCAPES

turned out to be from Iran and, indeed, lived in the camp. From the station, Ahmed, the Iraqi he befriended on the bus, and the Sudanese young men all walked for over an hour across town to the northern suburbs of Calais where the camp is located.

On November 3, 2015, at around 7:00pm (by then completely dark), Ahmed and his new friends arrived at the entrance of the Calais Jungle. He had been on the road for five months since leaving Sudan in early June. In those months, Ahmed crossed six countries and a sea. He was exhausted and penniless, but he was also thrilled beyond words. Many of his fellow African migrants had been robbed, beaten, or arrested during their journeys. Countless others perished at sea. Upon entering the camp, Ahmed thanked Allah for getting him there safely. Arrival at the Jungle, however, was not the end of Ahmed's story. Indeed, his fight for survival in one of the most notorious migrant camps in the world had just begun.

————————

It is Christmas Day. Much like the day before, Ahmed and I spend the afternoon walking around the camp, waiting for something to happen—something like a bad traffic jam that would send everyone in the camp running for the nearby highway. But it is Christmas; the highway is almost deserted. So, the waiting game continues. There is not much else to do here except hope. After several days, it has finally stopped raining, but a thick, gloomy fog has settled over everything in sight. Incessant coughing from the camp's residents fills the air. I ask Ahmed if the rough living conditions shocked him when he first arrived. He says he had spent many hours in cyber cafés in Italy and Germany doing research online about what to expect once he got to the Jungle. He even watched YouTube videos of the camp to

mentally prepare himself. He tells me that he was ready for the cold weather, ready to sleep in tents, ready to soldier through on just one meal a day. What he had not anticipated, however, was not being able to shower more than once a week. That, he says, is the one thing about life in the camp he finds hardest to deal with. "And we hardly wash our clothes," he adds, clearly frustrated by the poor sanitation. "Once we wash them, they take forever to dry."

I press him a bit harder: Why the Jungle? Ahmed says his destination had always been Britain. He has relatives in London and Bristol and it is where he says he has the best chance of achieving his goals. The Calais Jungle is the only possible gateway to the UK for people without a visa. I ask him if he ever considered applying for asylum in France? His answer is an emphatic no. Ahmed says he would rather go anywhere else in Europe than settle in France. Yes, his living conditions would improve dramatically. He would be taken out of the camp and placed in a refugee center somewhere in France (asylum seekers have no choice in where they are placed) and he would be given a warm room, a clean bed, and regular meals. But there is a high price to pay for that relative comfort. The process of obtaining asylum can take upwards of two years, and if his claim is rejected, which happens often, he will be deported from the country. To make matters worse, for that entire period he is waiting for a decision on his asylum claim, he would not be able to go anywhere or do anything except eat and sleep, and perhaps go to a language school for a couple of hours a day if he is lucky.

Also, by applying for asylum here in France, he would forfeit his right to claim asylum anywhere else in the EU. The strict, so-called Dublin Regulation prohibits what is pejoratively called "asylum shopping," seeking asylum in more than one EU country. Even if he manages to endure several years of living in a refugee center and is granted asylum, he would end up with a permit to stay in France legally for ten years and, after that time, be told to fend for himself. "Without money, without language, what do you do?" he asks me, not rhetorically but out of bewilderment at his predicament. Ahmed answers his own question. "You become homeless in Paris. That's not a life. That is not a future."

Ahmed tells me he did not travel all this way to watch TV, eat and sleep with no chance of escape for two years. He refuses to trade stagnation in Somaliland for stagnation in Europe. At least here, in the camp, he lives with hope. Even if rare, the chance of escape is ever present. Ahmed is convinced that one day he will sneak into a truck and finally make it to England.

Ahmed refers to himself as "mustaqbal raadis." It is a Somali phrase that roughly translates to "future-seeker." Unlike many African migrants who claim, honestly or otherwise, that they are fleeing human rights abuses or terrorist organizations such as Boko Haram, Ahmed is candid about why he has come to Europe. "I was not fleeing war or conflict," he says. "I just wanted a better future." In Ahmed's eyes, the only way to secure the future he has been seeking since he left Hargeisa is to sneak into one of those UK-bound cargo trucks. The more time I spend with Ahmed, the more the fact that he is "a man waiting for a train"—to what he sees as his promised land—strikes me. It lies so tantalizingly close, just on the other side of a body of water so narrow he could walk across it in about ten hours were such a thing possible.

Since Ahmed arrived at the camp, he has treated what he calls "trying my luck" as a full-time occupation. Before his hand was broken, he used to try his luck almost every day. He would walk for two hours in the hope of finding an unfenced bit of the highway so he could sneak into the back of a truck during a traffic jam. The extremely low odds of making it safely across the English Channel never deter him. If anything, this seems to fuel his resolve. Ahmed

tells me that he has been detected by every means available to authorities. One time, he was called out by barking dogs as he hid among crates of alcohol in the back of a transport truck. Another time, he managed to get into a truck that drove all the way to the entrance of the tunnel complex before. The large x-ray scanners designed to detect body heat, through which all UK bound trucks must pass, spotted Ahmed.

With all these opportunities for detection, the chance for migrants like Ahmed to get anywhere near the tunnel has become nearly nonexistent. As a result, more of them are staying in the camp much longer than they ever planned. Many of the camp residents I speak to have been living there for a year, some of them for two. But this has done little to deter residents from trying their luck. In September 2015, a freight train killed an Eritrean man as he attempted to walk through the tunnel. To dissuade more camp residents from trying this particularly deadly means of crossing the channel, the French authorities have promised harsh prison sentences for anyone caught trying to enter the tunnel on foot. The other crime that results in jail time is the cutting of the miles of fences that surround the camp, the port, and the tunnel. Anyone seen cutting the fences can face up to six months in prison, then deportation.

Arrests and deportations are not the only dangers the migrants face as they try to escape the camp. The most common thing that the residents do is climb over the fences, something that has caused a great deal of injuries, and in some cases even death. The fences are almost twenty feet high and topped with barbed wire. To avoid cutting themselves, some of the men take blankets or sleeping bags, climb up and cover the wire with them. It is usually at this point that some of the men fall from the fence, breaking bones, and sustaining head injuries.

Ahmed tells me that Yusuf, a good friend of his

from Darfur, died as he was trying to get to the other side of the fence. He had managed to successfully scale the fence along the highway, Ahmed says, but just as he was climbing down the other side, a patrol van arrived and two police officers chased him. As Yusuf was running across the highway, an oncoming car hit him. The driver never stopped. The French authorities took Yusuf's body for autopsy, and Ahmed and other Muslim residents in the camp performed the Janazah, the Muslim funeral prayer, without the body. Customarily, the Janazah prayer is performed in front of the deceased but since this was not possible, they had to conduct the prayer without Yusuf's remains. Ahmed says he does not know if his friend was given a proper Muslim burial by the French government. For Ahmed, the worst part of Yusuf's death was not being able to contact Yusuf's family back in Darfur. Without a telephone number, an email or street address for Yusuf's people, he had no way of letting them know he had died so far from home.

Even after having his hand broken by the French police and losing a close friend, Ahmed feels he is in exactly the right place. It is just a matter of waiting for the right time. One of the many remarkable things that struck me about Ahmed is the clarity of his ambition. He has a crystal-line vision and will not let go, even if it means enduring the countless indignities of living in a squalid migrant camp. Another thing that sets Ahmed apart from the many other young men I meet here is his utter lack of self-pity. In the five days we spend together, not once do I see him despondent or even melancholy at the situation he finds himself in. Nor do I see in him the rage I witness in some of the other men, such as Omar, a twenty-one-year-old Sudanese man whose first words to me are, "Fuck France!" Within minutes of meeting him, Omar tells me how much he hates France and the French people. He even resents that the camp is so widely known as the Jungle. "We are not animals!" he seethes.

Ahmed also does not exhibit the blind, almost childish optimism that I see in Hassan, a thirty-two-year-old man also from Sudan, who has lived in the camp for two years. Hassan told me his "dreams have been sleeping." So many of the young African men I meet in the camp seem genuinely surprised by the gulf between the Europe of their imaginations and the realities they encounter once they get here. Listening to their stories, it is hard not to feel as though they, unlike Ahmed, have done next to no research or planning before embarking on a potentially lethal journey. Their naiveté about the ways of the world is at once shocking and heartbreaking.

At sunset, the temperature drops precipitously. Unrelenting winds shake tents and send trash flying around us. Cold rain falls sideways, hitting us in the face as we try to navigate the muddy roads. On our way, we pass the many high fences that enclose the compound. Under one of the fences is a large, hand-written sign designed by the camp residents. It reads, "We Have a Dream," as if to remind the people who built these fences that the collective dreams of thousands of migrants and refugees are more resilient than any barbed wire fence.

Drenched and cold, Ahmed and I finally make it to the Sudanese tent, one of the largest in the camp, where Ahmed spends most of his time. This evening, the tent is abuzz with activity. Newly-donated single beds arrived that afternoon; the residents are busy getting rid of the old beds and assembling the new ones. About sixty beds are placed so close to one another that there is barely any room to walk around the large tent. A din of laughter and Arabic music from a small radio fills the air, as well as smoke from a stove upon which one of the residents makes dinner from canned foods donated by a local NGO.

After the cleanup, as I drink the sweet, milky tea that I have been offered, I listen to several of the residents' stories about life in the camp. The most eloquent of the men is Bushar Ahmed from Sudan. He is thirty-three years old and has been in Calais since the summer of 2015. He tells me that he lives in a much smaller camp in the woods not far from the main camp, and that he only comes to the larger camp for food and showers. He chooses to stay in the smaller camp because it is in the forest and the CRS police rarely go there. Everyone I speak to is petrified of the CRS police.

Although most residents have a disturbing story of police brutality, Bushar seems to have witnessed more than most. He says he once saw a migrant being chased by the police after trying to board a truck. As the man was running, he fell into a large drainage canal (of which there are many around Calais). The man did not know how to swim, and Bushar claims that the French police watched him drown. Bushar says he also witnessed his own friend, with whom he traveled all the way from Sudan, get hit by a car on the highway while running from the police. Bushar believes that his friend would still be alive if the French police had not pepper-sprayed him just beforehand, severely impairing his vision. Bushar was devastated to watch his friend die right in front of him, but death, he says, is something he is used to. He had experienced more deaths than he can count in the Sahara Desert while journeying to Europe. There is not enough time to mourn each death, he says, his voice devoid of emotion. "You just move on."

Moving on, it seems, is a way of life for all the African migrants I meet. Almost all of them came to Europe by way of the Sahara, where death in the form of starvation, dehydration, and violence is ever present. However, the danger posed by the desert pales in comparison to that of the Mediterranean Sea. By the end of December 2016, five thousand people perished at sea according to the International Organization for Migration's Missing Migrant Project, which has been tracking migrant

deaths around the world for many years. For those lucky enough to survive the crossing, nightmares of the sea often linger long after. I discovered this when I traveled to Italy which, for all intents and purposes, serves as the gateway to Europe for almost all African migrants.

———

The boat is taking in water. Nine hours have passed since it left land. It is November, and the water is freezing. Dozens of the 450 people on board are cramped in the bottom hull. Thirty-three-year-old Kamal, from Eritrea, is one of them. He is cold. All he has on are a pair of old pants and a t-shirt. Large waves continually slam against the boat as more water pours in. The boat leans to one side and everyone in the hull moves in the opposite direction to counteract the weight of the water. The boat sways violently. As he hears the terrified screams of the people around him, Kamal is scared for his life. He has, after all, seen television news footage of lifeless African bodies being fished from the sea. He remembers asking his smugglers for a life-jacket before they left Libya. The smuggler's answer: "Italia will give you."

The Mediterranean Sea is a graveyard. About 70 percent of the 7,189 migrant deaths recorded worldwide in 2016 occurred in the Mediterranean, according to the Missing Migrant Project. Most of the dead are African asylum seekers attempting to cross the choppy, freezing waters in rickety boats. At times, there can be as many as nine hundred souls in a single vessel. Most of these deaths take place during peak migration season, which falls between April and November. Many of the dead get buried in unmarked graves in villages and towns along the Mediterranean, their names, and histories no one will ever know, their hopes and dreams forever lost to the sea. As for the lucky ones, like Kamal, who survive the crossing, a dizzying array of new ordeals await.

The vast majority of African migrants who make it safely to Europe are designated "economic migrants" in search of jobs and a better life, reasons that are not recognized by European Union immigration laws as legitimate grounds for asylum. Most economic migrants languish in identification centers on islands such as Lampedusa and Sicily, or in reception houses in cities like Naples. Thousands more continue their northward marches to wealthy European countries such as Germany, Norway and Britain.

Up on a hill, away from the congested, dilapidated streets of old Naples, sitting atop Via Marechiaro, is a two-story pink mansion overlooking the Gulf of Naples below. With its impressive, well-kept gardens and million-dollar views of the sea and the city, one can be forgiven for mistaking this place as the home of a movie star, not a guesthouse for destitute African migrants.

At the foot of steep stairs adorned with potted pink flowers, Ottavio Balzano, a lanky, twenty-eight-year-old with a rumpled green shirt and a messy mane of brown hair, greets me warmly. Balzano is an administrator here and has agreed to show me around the grand property. Upon entering the main hall of the house, I am struck by the contrast of the lush exterior and the drab quarters within. The poorly lit entrance hall is austere. A single desk sits in the middle of the room. A small wooden cross is hanging on the wall. Next to the entrance hall is another dim room where a group of seven residents are watching a soccer match on a small television. They barely notice us as Balzano tells me about the house. There are twenty-four adult residents in total: fourteen young men and ten women, three of them with infant babies. They all are from African countries such as Mali, Nigeria, Cameroon and Senegal.

A narrow staircase leads up to sleeping quarters comprising ten bedrooms, two-to-four guests to a room. I ask Balzano if I can see the bedrooms. With an embarrassed laugh, he declines. It was hard enough to convince the manager of the house to let me visit in the first place, he says. "They want journalists," he notes wryly, "but, like, the right journalists."

"What is the right journalist?" I ask.

"The ones they call," Balzano says with a snort.

The "they" he's refereeing to is Laity Third World (LTM), the NGO that runs the reception center. LTM is funded by the European Union through the Italian government. Balzano leads me to his office, which is cluttered with binders, paperwork, and boxes of everything from toiletries to coffee and tea for the residents.

The reluctance of LTM to have journalists poking around its guesthouse is understandable. Numerous corruption scandals involving migrant reception centers like this have hit the international media in recent years. Most of the cases involved organizations that won lucrative contracts from the Italian government to house and feed the hundreds of thousands of migrants who have illegally entered Italy in recent years. The last two years are particularly noteworthy.

According to the International Organization for Migration, as of December 2016, 179,523 migrants and refugees came to the shores of Italy. In 2015, the number was 153,842.

To deal with the staggering number of asylum seekers, the Italian government regularly puts out calls to private institutions, individuals and NGOs that can accommodate them. In return, the Italian government pays the bill to the tune of one billion euros a year. The state gives any NGO or property owner thirty-five euros a day for each migrant they host. Many hotel owners across southern Italy, who were hit hard by the 2009 debt crisis and the resulting tourism slump, have opened their establishments to cash in on the growing business of housing migrants. In exchange for the thirty-five euros per head that the government pays, hosts must guarantee the migrants basic services such as housing and food, as stipulated by EU asylum laws.

Outsourcing of government services like this has been a boon to unscrupulous businessmen looking to make a quick buck. There have been many media reports of private reception houses without heat, running water or even working toilets. The situation in some of these centers was so dire the government declared them unfit for human habitation and shut them down. The most shocking case of corruption and abuse in Italy's private reception homes is the infamous "Mafia Capitale" scandal. According to reports, an alliance of corrupt government officials and mafia figures worked together to allegedly swindle millions from the government. One of the defendants at the center of that case, Salvatore Buzzi, whose trail started in November 2015, was heard in a wiretap conversation boasting that "drugs were less profitable than the business of housing asylum seekers."[5]

"This is a small house. Here you can easily take care of people properly," Balzano tells me in a slightly defensive tone. "This is considered, like, the best place in Naples."

He may well be right. Considering the horrendous living conditions in some of the migrant houses that have been reported in the media, what I have seen of this residence is clean and orderly.

However, nothing can hide the sense of quiet desperation and hopelessness that permeates the air. Although EU laws governing the treatment of asylum seekers stipulate that new arrivals wishing to apply for asylum in Italy be entitled to have their cases heard in immigration courts within thirty to sixty days, the process can take over two years. As designed, the system should

be simple and timely. Every new person who comes into Italy illegally is processed in large reception centers where they are fingerprinted and distributed among available guest houses in cities like Palermo and Naples. Eventually, they are seen by immigration lawyers who help them prepare for hearings before a group of judges who ultimately decide the fate of each migrant.

If they are accepted, then they are deemed legitimate political asylum seekers, a designation reserved for those fleeing war, state-sponsored violence and political persecution. This comes with a permit to stay in the country legally. Eritrea is one of only a handful of African countries whose people have traditionally been given asylum by EU Member States. According to Eurostat, generally about 90 percent of Eritreans are granted asylum by EU countries. However, the unofficial list of countries granted asylum keeps changing as political situations in these nations evolve. For decades, those fleeing civil wars from Somalia and South Sudan were traditionally given refugee status. Since the end of civil war in Somalia and the establishment of the independent state of South Sudan, migrants from these countries have been lumped with other Africans from countries such as Nigeria, Mali and Ethiopia. They rarely qualify for refugee status. A special exception is sometimes made for LGBT members fleeing religious persecution in their countries.

A great deal of the debate about the current migration crisis has centered on just how to describe the people involved. Refugees? Asylum seekers? Economic migrants? These classifications may be important for immigration law purposes, but they over-simply what is a more complex human drama.

According to the United Nations High Commissioner for Refugees (UNHCR), as of mid-2016, sixty-five million people have been forcibly displaced from their home countries. These tens of millions of people are displaced for a variety of reasons—everything from civil wars, as in the case of Syria, to political or religious persecution, as in the case of Rohingya Muslims in Myanmar. There are also people fleeing countries where political repression is so bad, like in Eritrea, that many people flee in search of freedom. To further complicate matters, there are also those fleeing terrorism and severe economic hardships as a result of recently ended civil wars. Separating these millions of people into neat categories of refugees and migrants is often arbitrary. According to the strict, internationally accepted standards of the Refugee Convention of 1951, only about twenty-one million of the sixty-five million currently displaced people are recognized as refugees because they are fleeing active armed conflict or political persecution. To add another layer of complexity, there is the problem of legitimate refugees who arrive in countries like Greece or Italy, but then cross numerous borders within the EU in search of a wealthier country in which to reside. Since they are not abiding by the so-called "first safe country" principle of the Refugee Convention, which dictates that refugees fearing for their lives should seek asylum in the first safe country in which they land, they risk automatically losing their protections as refugees for the mere fact of wanting to improve their future economic prospects.

Migrants, on the other hand, are people whose lives are not in imminent danger but who, according to the Refugee Convention, have left their homelands to "improve their lives by finding work, or in some cases for education, family reunion, or other reasons." Ahmed, the Somali in earlier sections of this story, is a good example. However, real life is often far too complex to fit into simple classifications. Most international law experts concede that many people engaged in the current migration crisis in Europe can simultaneously be refugees and migrants. Anyone fleeing countries like South Sudan, parts of Ethiopia, Mali, Eastern Nigeria and parts of Somalia might fit the bill. In these

cases, recently ended armed conflicts may have all but destroyed the economic and education systems of a country, while low-grade conflicts make life almost unlivable, especially for young people.

Baby-faced and soft spoken, Torey Ibrahim might easily be mistaken for a fifteen-year-old were it not for his powerfully athletic physique. He is eighteen, from Mali. In 2014, he embarked on a dangerous three-week journey across the Sahara Desert in a four-by-four jeep with a group of other young men. For five months, Torey stayed in Tripoli, where he routinely fought with Libyan gangs who tried to rob him of whatever possessions he had. On one occasion, when they could not find any money on him, they took his cellphone and shirt.

After working for five months in a butcher shop, Torey finally had the 2,000 Libyan dinars (the equivalent of $1,400); he needed to pay traffickers to get him across the Mediterranean to Europe. The journey took just over twenty-four hours. On a small fishing boat with almost thirty others (and no life vests), Torey was lucky enough to arrive safely. On August 30, 2014, the boat he was in was intercepted by an Italian rescue ship, and everyone on board was taken to an island in Southern Italy (the name of which Torey cannot remember).

"I left Mali because there is a very serious war there," Torey tells me. "There are many groups of terrorists."

For years now, various insurgent groups such as the Islamic Movement for Azawad and Al-Qaeda in the Islamic Maghreb have been waging deadly attacks in Mali against the Western-backed government. But it is civilians who suffer most at the hands of these groups. Torey says the terrorist groups order young men to join them. Otherwise, these young men and their families become targets for violence. His claims are hard to verify, but they sound like what other terror groups such as Al-Shabaab have been doing in Somalia: giving young men of Torey's age a "you're with us or against us" ultimatum.

Making it big in Italy as a professional football player, where so many African players before him have become global superstars, was a dream that sustained Torey even in his darkest days in Libya. Ottavio Balzano says that Torey is a gifted player with extraordinary natural talent. However, he has most likely missed that small window of opportunity where natural talent must receive the required training and resources to succeed. Most young men who go on to become professional football players have to be in prestigious training camps by their early- or mid-teens to even have a decent shot at the professional leagues.

When he is not at school trying to learn enough Italian in hopes of one day getting a job, Torey spends most of his days perfecting his soccer skills at a nearby field without the guidance of a coach. The week before I met him, Torey finally had his appointment with the immigration commission, and with the help of a lawyer, made his case for asylum in Italy. He is awaiting the commission's verdict. It could be years before one arrives. In the meantime, the waiting continues.

For every Torey who claims to be fleeing the clutches of ruthless terror groups, there are many African migrants who do not even bother to hide their real reason for coming to Europe. Many of them regard it as the land of economic prosperity—a modern day El Dorado. The combination of disparate groups of people fleeing for so many different reasons—not to mention the sheer magnitude of the exodus from Africa—have created huge backlogs of cases with tens of thousands of claimants and not enough immigration lawyers and judges to handle them. However, Balzano puts some of the blame on his country. "Italy is just not

organized enough for this kind of bureaucratic work," he says. "Even if we had twenty years, we would still be processing the current cases."

Balzano says that, at some point, the waiting starts weighing heavily on the residents and adds to the sense of confusion inherent in confronting a labyrinthine legal system. "It's very hard to know their state of mind," Balzano continues. "They're not open, but they're very emotional . . . and I think they're very confused." He explains that, although many of the residents have been through a series of migrant detention centers on islands like Lampedusa and Sicily, by the time they come to this house, their traumatic experiences of crossing the Sahara Desert or the Mediterranean Sea, or both, continue to haunt them.

"Some of them are really, really desperate, and some of them are really confused," Balzano says. "I have read their files and their stories, but for me, it's very difficult to understand."

How do they get along among themselves?

"We have a lot of issues about Wi-Fi relations. They fight about it . . ."

It may sound baffling to be fighting about Wi-Fi, given the larger predicaments these residents face, but access to the Internet is crucial for their sanity. Websites like YouTube are often the only source of entertainment the residents have. It is also through Facebook and WhatsApp that they keep in touch with their loved ones back home. More disturbing to Balzano are the incidents of domestic violence between the few couples in the house. There are three couples, and each couple has an infant baby. Balzano recounts one incident:

"Once, I was here alone and one girl came running in here and hid behind me, and then the husband came and they started to fight. The girl said "don't leave, he's going to kill me."

There was physical violence between this couple before, but if I wasn't there that day for sure …" Balzano's voice trails off, as if to contemplate the countless horrific scenarios that might have been. "I went upstairs with her and her baby, but I didn't press charges. . . . You don't solve the problem by calling the police. You can divide a family, and the woman doesn't want this. They have a very violent life story, and you have to deal with it," he explains. "You can't just say, 'I despise violence, so no violence here.' It doesn't work like that. They told me stories about Libya. It was like a living hell for them, and some of them have knife scars."

Once the residents leave the confines of the compound and go out into the city, what happens while there only adds to their stress. Due to its geography as a port, Naples has had a long and distinguished history of being a deeply multicultural city. Nevertheless, it is currently experiencing the same political and cultural backlash against migrants that has swept the rest of Italy and much of Europe. So, when the residents of the house go into the city for one of their doctor or lawyer appointments, locals sometimes accost them. He recounts an incident that took place when he accompanied a group of residents to the city

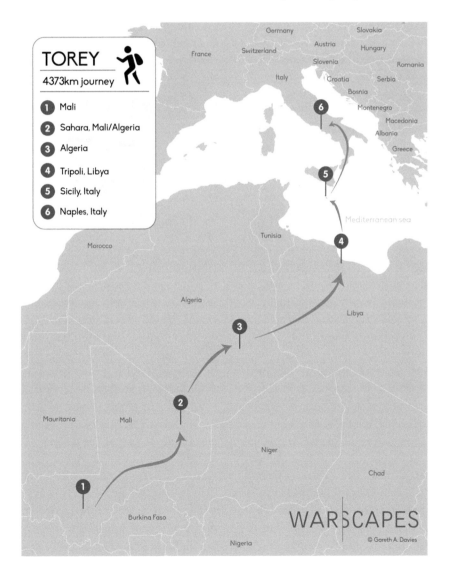

center for a cultural tour: They were repeatedly called names, told to go back to where they came from and that they smelled.

I ask Balzano what is fueling these racist attacks. He is quick to respond: "Television," he says. "Here they are talking every day on the television about how the immigrants are stealing money from us."

There is a deep anger not just in Naples, but across Italy, at the government for its inability to protect the country's borders. Absent a clear target for their animus, however, some Italians' most venomous anger is often directed at the African migrants, who many view as not only sucking up the country's resources but also driving away the tourism upon which many cities, towns and villages in Southern Italy depend. Italians opposed to immigration often claim that the migrants are not "real refugees," but rather people who have come to take advantage of the European system to better their economic circumstances.

"We're living in bondage because of the bad government," Immanuel Ufuku says in a hoarse voice. "I believe that in Europe, I can make it. That's why I'm here." Short, stocky, and with a bulging stomach that makes him look much older than a man in his mid-thirties, Immanuel, who hails from Nigeria, is likely what anti-immigration Italians picture when they think of an "economic migrant." He says he left the Delta region of Nigeria "because of bad government. No work. Nothing." He, too, made the perilous journey across the Sahara and the Mediterranean. The boat he was on carried 610 people. When I ask him why he put his life in such danger, his answer is quick: "Without risk, you cannot live." That seems to be the motto of most the migrants I meet. They seem to possess extraordinary faith in the simple act of risk-taking—risk and God. "If God says yes, nobody can say no!" Immanuel proclaims with the zeal of a TV evangelist.

Immanuel is equally blunt about why he is at the house. "In Italy, there is no work. . . . When I get my documents, then I will go to Sweden." Immanuel is not fleeing war or persecution, but rather economic troubles so severe that he would rather risk death than stay in his country. Compared to desperate Syrian parents fleeing bombs with children in tow, many Europeans find it hard to feel any sympathy for people like Immanuel.

What makes Immanuel even more unsympathetic in their eyes, perhaps, is that he knows how to game the system. He understands he has almost no chance of success with the immigration commission if he tells them that he came to Europe in search of work. Instead, he says he will tell them that he is running away from Boko Haram, the notorious Islamist terror group in North Eastern Nigeria that has made international headlines with its brutal attacks on civilians and school girls. The fact that Immanuel is from the Delta region in Southern Nigeria, an area unaffected by Boko Haram's brutality, does not seem to concern him. All that matters to him is getting to Sweden, or maybe Canada, where he says he has dreamt of going all his life. Later, he seems to spin the globe again, telling me: "I cannot wait for my feet to touch America. . . . I love America!"

Sweden, Canada, America—for Immanuel they are all the same—interchangeable, wealthy Western countries where financial success is all but guaranteed, if he can find a way to get there. It is not clear how Immanuel plans to legally settle in Sweden. Neither is it clear how he is going to get to Canada or the United States. Reality does not seem to matter much to men like Immanuel; like a gambler, visions of hitting the jackpot seem to blind him to the odds against him.

It is late in the day and the setting sun casts long shadows on the immaculately kept compound gardens. Just before I leave, Balzano tells me in a quiet voice, as if to let me in on a secret, that most of the migrants who live in the house have almost no chance of being granted asylum in Italy. Once they are denied permission to stay in the country legally, they can submit to being moved to the Identification and Expulsion Centers, more commonly known as CIEs, which Balzano makes clear is "not a place you want to go."

CIE centers have more in common with maximum-security prisons than immigration detention centers. They have become quite common across Italy as a sort of holding place before migrants who are deemed ineligible for asylum and ordered to be expelled from the country. However, detainees at these centers are almost comically referred to as "guests." I have seen many photographs of CIE centers in Italy, such as the haunting pictures taken by the Italian photojournalist Mario Badagliacca, and I would argue that these centers are essentially internment camps. Violent riots and mental health troubles such as depression and anxiety are common, and so is the occasional suicide. In 2013, the Italian NGO Doctors for Human Rights published a report—"The CIE Archipelago—Inquiry into the Italian Centres for Identification and Expulsion"—derived from a year-long study of CIE centers across Italy. The report concluded that these centers are "congenitally incapable of safeguarding respect for an individual's dignity and basic human rights."

The only other option available to the residents of the house is to head north, using a complex network of transportation, to try their luck at sneaking into countries like Germany, Norway or the most popular, Great Britain. To get there, they will have to embark on yet another risky journey to transportation hubs like Rome or Milan, where there are few services for migrants on the move. To survive, they will have to rely on the kindness of strangers at informal migration centers, places like the now-closed Baobab Migration Centre in Rome.

———

"I want to be free in my country, to talk about the economic situation, about the political situation, about the social situation," Kamal, the Eritrean migrant I met, tells me as he buttons up his brown jacket against the cold sweeping over Rome in recent days. "It's my right to talk!" he continues, indignant. "My mother and father [were] fighters for independence in Eritrea. My father is a martyr for the country, for democracy, for justice, for freedom."

We stand on the side of Via Cupa, a tiny street that runs in front of The Baobab Migration Centre not far from Tiburtina Station, one of Rome's biggest train and bus terminals where many migrants first set foot in the Italian capital. Despite being closed by the local government on December 6, 2015, a few weeks after the Paris terrorist attacks, the Baobab Centre continues to be a gathering place for many migrants from Southern Italy who are on the move, in search of a better life in the UK and elsewhere in Northern Europe. The words "Protect People Not Borders" are scrawled in big black letters on the front wall of the center, a large, beige-colored villa that looks as run-down as the Colosseum.

Listening to Kamal speak about what he calls "the harsh life of Eritreans" with such passion and sadness, it is quite evident that he is a highly intelligent, politically engaged man who might have been a leader of some opposition political party had he lived in a country where such a thing was allowed. If Eritrea ever had an Arab Spring-style revolution, Kamal would surely have been on the frontlines. Kamal has only been in Rome for three weeks. He is now thirty-three years old; he left Eritrea when he was twenty-nine. After serving in the national army for one month, a compulsory service for young Eritrean men, he made the hard decision to leave his country. He did not want to end up like one of his friends who served in the military for nineteen years for an annual salary of 1,000 nakfa, the equivalent of about $450, a fate Kamal likens to slavery.

Eritrea is one of the poorest countries in Africa because it had nearly been destroyed by three decades of war for independence with its much larger and more powerful neighbor, Ethiopia. Ever since its independence in 1991, the tiny nation on the Red Sea has remained in a constant state of combat-readiness, which demands of its young people indefinite service in the military. As a result, Eritrea has an army of "320,000, one the highest soldier-to-population ratios in the world."[6] This is one of the reasons why, for a country roughly the size of Ohio and with a population of about six million people, Eritrea produces, per capita, the highest number of migrants of any African country. The United Nations High Commissioner for Refugees (UNHCR) estimates that about "4,000 Eritreans flee the country each month and that as of mid-2014, 313,000 Eritreans—about 5 percent of the population—have fled."

"It's good to work for your country," Kamal says. "We are ready to die for our country. If Ethiopia came to our border, we are ready to die for Eritrea. But there must be fairness in the country." Kamal says the current political and economic situation, overseen by one of the world's most oppressive regimes, left him with no choice but to take a dangerous journey to Europe. His voyage included three years in a refugee camp in Sudan. As soon as he saved enough money to get himself across the Sahara, he headed to Libya, the most direct way into Europe for many of Africa's tens of thousands of migrants who undertake the same trip.

On the back of a pickup truck with about fifteen other migrants, Kamal spent five days crossing the desert. He says he was lucky; their journey was uneventful. For many, the trip can take as many as twenty days due to the harsh conditions of the roads. Cars frequently breakdown, water is scarce, and armed bandits roam free. The bandits are especially worrisome, robbing men and raping women who have the misfortunate of encountering them. For those lucky enough to safely cross the Sahara, Libya often turns out to be the most dangerous part of their journey. Many of the migrants I spoke to who came to Italy by way of Libya describe the country as a "nightmare" or "hell on earth." Kamal is no exception. He says when he arrived in Tripoli, the capital, members of an armed militia abducted him. Ever since 2011, following the violent overthrow of Muammar Gaddafi, who ruled the oil-rich nation for close to forty years, much of the country, including parts of the capital, have been effectively controlled by militias.

Kamal says he was held captive for four months, first in Sika Prison near Gaddafi's former palace. He was then taken to Salahadeen Prison on the outskirts of Tripoli, where Kamal claims to have been put in an underground cell with many other Eritreans and other Africans. Kamal recounts a period of mistreatment that included having his hair shaved by force, sleeping on the hard floor and having only two meals a day consisting of plain rice. He cups his palm to demonstrate the puny amount of rice he was given twice a day. Kamal also alleges that he witnessed prison guards open fire on men who tried to escape.

There have been many reported cases describing conditions like Kamal's accounts of abduction and abuse in Libya. Border police and armed gangs have created a criminal network there in which African migrants are detained by police, then handed over to gangs who hold them for ransom. The proceeds are divvied up between them. A report published in 2015 by Amnesty International, called "Libya is Full of Cruelty: Stories of Abduction, Sexual Violence and Abuse from Migrants and Refugees,"[7] recounted the harrowing testimonies of survivors. The only way for the abducted migrants to regain their freedom is to pay upwards of $500, a sum too high for these often-penniless people. Kamal gained his freedom thanks to a middleman who paid his captors the $500, a kind of "freedom loan," which he had to pay back with interest once he was released. These men who Kamal describes as businessmen recoup their money by giving cellphones to the migrants and telling them to call their families back home and ask them to wire the money. The distraught families are often forced to sell their cars, goats, cows and whatever other valuables they possess to buy the release of their loved ones.

In November 2015, once he managed to pay off the money he owed the middlemen, plus another $2,000 for the boat ride to Italy, Kamal undertook his dangerous journey across the Mediterranean. After nine hours at sea, he and the other 450 migrants on were rescued by a patrol ship belonging to Luxembourg, which was taking part in a humanitarian operation known as European Union Naval Force Mediterranean, nicknamed "Operation Sophia." From the sea, Kamal and the others were taken to a migrant processing center in the port of Pozzallo, in Sicily, where he was held for five days in a center he likens to a prison. When he was asked to be fingerprinted, Kamal refused. He knew the EU immigration process well enough to know that, if his fingerprints where taken in Italy, his chances of claiming asylum in any other EU country would be lost.

In addition to blocking the possibility of "asylum shopping," the Dublin Agreement also establishes a continent-wide fingerprinting database that makes tracking the movements of migrants easier for Frontex, an agency created to combat illegal migration. Like many of the EU migration laws, Dublin Agreement has failed to work as designed. Some financially strapped countries like Italy and Greece, which have been most affected by the migration crisis, often do

not fingerprint new arrivals and simply allow them to travel northward, thus freeing them from the financial burden of having to care for tens of thousands of migrants and refugees. Lax implementation of the Dublin Agreement allows people like Kamal to travel from port cities in Southern Italy, where they first land, to larger cities such as Turin, Milan, and Rome, where they often seek help in places like the Baobab Migration Centre.

It is just after five in the evening, and it is already dark and cold. Two large lights above the black gate of the now-locked Baobab Centre cast a warm orange glow over the entire area. A cacophony of Italian, Arabic, and Tigrigna, Eritrea's official language, fills the air. Dinner will not be served for another hour or so but there is already a steady stream of young men waiting for food. About fourteen or so migrants and five volunteers stand around waiting for food to be brought by volunteers who live in the neighborhood. There are no female migrants, just young men in ill-fitting, donated clothes.

The relatively small group of migrants waiting for warm meals on this cold December evening is very different from the huge numbers of people who used to stay here in the summer—the height of the migration season—when the Baobab Centre used to feed as many as 800 migrants in transit. Andrea Costa, the coordinator of volunteers at the center, tells me that the rooms of the center would be so full that migrants would sleep in tents and sleeping bags laid out in the large courtyard of the building. However, the number of new arrivals coming across the Mediterranean dwindles considerably in the winter months, when the sea is just too dangerous for small boats. Even with the closing of the center, they are still getting an average of five new arrivals every day. Costa estimates that in 2015 alone, about thirty-five thousand migrants in transit stayed here, most of them continuing their journey after a few days of much needed rest.

What makes the Baobab Centre remarkable is that even though it officially closed, it still manages to help countless migrants traveling through Rome on their way north. Another noteworthy thing about Baobab is that it is entirely volunteer-run. Donations of food and clothes come from citizens and NGOs, and all the people who work here are volunteers with full-time jobs. Costa, for instance, runs a store not far from the center where he restores stained glass windows. The volunteers coordinate their shifts on a Facebook page they created. There is also another Facebook page called "Friends of Baobab" where volunteers communicate with locals who wish to donate. If there is a need for toothpaste, for example, one of the volunteers will post a message to the locals and the next day boxes of toothpaste arrive. The same goes for socks or gloves or whatever else is needed. It is a haphazard system that could never match the resources of a government-run operation, but the volunteers somehow manage to meet the most urgent needs of the migrants.

Ever since the center officially closed at the direction of the local government and the arrival of winter, providing a place to sleep for the migrants has become a routine nightmare of frantic phone calls. Every evening after dinner, the volunteers conduct a headcount and make phone calls to homeless shelters and any other allies who may have spare beds. When the usual places, such as the Red Cross shelter or the city run homeless shelters, are full, volunteers have to get creative and call upon their personal networks. The night before, about ten of the boys had to sleep in an indoor basketball court. A few others slept at the offices of a left-wing political party that advocates for refugee rights.

Despite the closure of the center and the volunteers' limited resources, the Baobab Centre has developed a reputation, largely through word of mouth among refugees, as a port of safe sanctuary in Rome. Aside from warm meals and clothes, the center also acts as a gathering place where migrants socialize and exchange ideas about their journeys. They also receive medical help. A Doctors for Human Rights truck comes by almost every day ferrying volunteer doctors who provide treatment for minor injuries and ailments. The doctors also act as a kind of information point for those on their way to Germany, France, or England. Migrants receive the most up to date tips on which borders are closed, which crossings are the easiest and the locations of help centers along the way.

It is a week before Christmas and the streets of Rome are filled with families and shoppers getting ready for the holiday. But at the gate of the Baobab Migration Centre, this day is no different than any other. Volunteers are busy preparing meals as a group of fifteen young men or so, mostly from Eritrea and Morocco, mill around. Three boys who seem no older than fifteen play an improvised game of soccer in the narrow street in front of the center. Informal exercise is one of the best ways to keep warm during cold nights like this one.

Two new boys arrived a few hours ago. They were given donated coats, socks and some food. They sit, now, in orange plastic chairs against the wall and stare into space. They are both from Ethiopia and do not speak a word of English. Through a translator, I ask them a few questions, but they can hardly speak, their voices weak, their eyes expressionless. Aside from the two new arrivals the atmosphere this evening is jovial. Some of the volunteers brought chips and cookies. A fire roars in a large metal can around which a handful of Moroccan boys warm their hands. One of the Moroccans, who now lives in a "proper" shelter, has returned to socialize with friends. Pulling out an acoustic guitar, he entertains the crowd with ebullient Arabic tunes.

Just like his time in Sudan and Libya, Kamal maintains that Italy, too, is just another

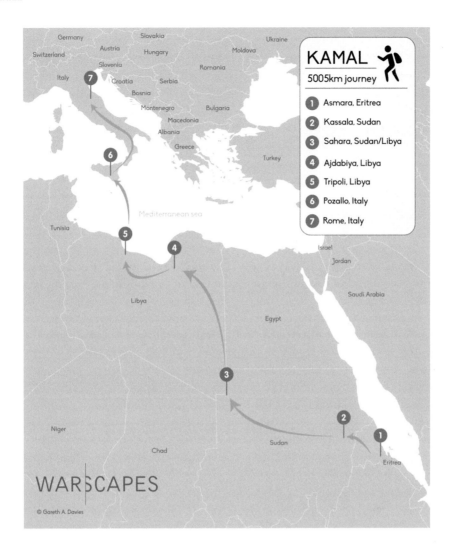

KAMAL

5005km journey

1. Asmara, Eritrea
2. Kassala, Sudan
3. Sahara, Sudan/Libya
4. Ajdabiya, Libya
5. Tripoli, Libya
6. Pozallo, Italy
7. Rome, Italy

WARSCAPES

© Gareth A. Davies

stopover in his long journey to freedom. He tells me, with a certainty that makes it almost impossible to doubt him, that he will get to his destination of Norway, where he has relatives and friends. He is at the planning stages of his trek there via Germany, where he has few Eritrean friends to help him along the way. I ask him if it has all been worth it: Three years in a refugee camp in Sudan; four months of captivity in Libya; and now being homeless in Rome.

"I know this is a dangerous situation," Kamal responds after taking a while to consider my question.

"But what do we do?" After another long pause,

he sums up: "Without freedom, what can we do?"

Two days later, on a sunny but frigid afternoon, I meet Kamal again at the gate of the Baobab Centre. He tells me that he has purchased a bus ticket to Milan. He seems excited by his impending trip, yet in his eyes it is hard to miss a certain apprehension. We both know that he is about to embark on another dangerous journey that could result in his being jailed and deported. When he finally starts his voyage, he will join thousands of fellow African migrants and refugees who travel across Western Europe by foot, bus, and train, illegally traversing what was intended to be a "borderless continent" thanks to the Schengen Agreement, which was signed in 1985 at a historic summit in the picturesque town of Schengen, Luxembourg. The Schengen Agreement was envisioned by a small group of forward thinking European diplomats who dreamed of a more open, peaceful, borderless Europe. It seems their revolutionary idea did not foresee the arrival of hundreds of thousands of refugees and migrants from the Southern Hemisphere—migrants fleeing war, political persecution, and poverty.

When he gets to Milan, Kamal will most likely land at Milano Centrale, the northern Italian city's central station, where he will find other young migrants from Africa. Train stations, from Tiburtina Station in Rome to Gare du Nord in Paris, are popular congregation points. These migrant men and women often have with them nothing more than a backpack or a plastic bag in which they carry the entirety of their possessions. If you observe them conversing long enough, you can usually see them exchange contact information or make plans to meet at various forward locations along their journeys. There seems to be, between them, a genuine sense of cooperation rather than competition. This is surprising, considering their precarious existence, especially as they continue their march from Africa to Northern Europe, and in so many cases, the Calais Jungle.

———

Calais has a storied past that goes back to the Middle Ages. In the seventeenth century, it was an important maritime city. More recently, during World War II, it was the scene of intense fighting and was virtually destroyed by the Germans. The city's fortunes improved after the war, but it gradually became a symbol of industrial decline in the last few decades like the decline in manufacturing that transformed major American cities in states like Ohio, Pennsylvania, and Michigan. Today, Calais has

become one of the poorest cities in France. Since 2008, the current mayor, Natasha Bouchard, has tried hard to exploit the nearby beaches and the city's rich history to rejuvenate Calais and turn it into a tourist destination. Bouchard has had little success, however. Most people here blame the historic migration drama unfolding in their backyard.

There is widespread feeling that the Jungle's myriad migrants have caused severe damage to the local economy. Right-wing parties, such as the National Front, which has been gaining support in the region, have successfully capitalized on local fears about mass migration. Unfortunately for the residents of Calais, the same geographic features that made their city an ideal site for tourism and a transportation hub have also made it a magnet for illegal migrants.

Today, the Jungle may be gone, but one of the big unknowns so far—a question not only for France, but the whole of Europe—concerns the long-term ramifications of the migration crisis currently unfolding. The massive influx of refugees and migrants has presented the continent with its biggest refugee crisis since World War II. But the crisis has been so deep and so wide in the number of countries impacted that it is beginning to threaten the very notion of the European Union. As Britain struggles with its exit from the EU following the 2016 Brexit referendum, which was animated considerably by the issue of Europe's refugee crisis, the fear is that other EU countries will also abandon the union. There is even talk of abandoning the much-heralded Schengen Agreement.

Some Southern states like Greece, Italy, and to a lesser extent, Spain, have withstood the worst of the crisis. Greece has been threatened with expulsion from the EU for not doing enough to stem the flow of asylum seekers from the Middle East, who are using Greece as a gateway into the rest of the continent. EU diplomats in Brussels have accused Greece of failing to process refugees and migrants properly, including setting up camps where they could be screened for security before being relocated to other countries. These hardest hit countries, however, contend that they have no choice but to let asylum seekers travel through to other EU countries. Their capacity to deal with tens of thousands of new refugees and migrants arriving every month has been overwhelmed, and the financial and logistical help they get from Brussels has not been commensurate with the scale of the crisis.

The migration crisis has exposed deep fissures between EU member states as each nation looks out for its own interests. For the first time since the Schengen Agreement came into effect, EU countries are publicly expressing the need to reconsider the open border aspect of the entire EU project. In January 2016, when EU interior ministers met in Amsterdam to discuss solutions to the migrant crisis, there were calls by some countries to immediately close the borders. Under existing rules, governments can temporarily suspend the open border clause in the agreement for national security emergencies. France, for example, did this following the November 2015 terrorist attacks in Paris. Following France's decision to close its borders, other countries including Sweden, Denmark and Germany also reintroduced border controls. Poland, Romania, and Bulgaria, among others, are considering similar moves.

Due to the unrelenting numbers of asylum seekers coming to Europe from the east in Greece and from the south across the Mediterranean Sea, coupled with the terror attacks in Paris, Nice, and Brussels, EU officials are making increasingly dire pronouncements about the future of Schengen. Some have warned that if the open border agreement is allowed to collapse, it could bring about the dissolution of the union altogether. The end of the Schengen would be not just the demise of a unique bureaucratic experiment, but something far graver. It would

amount to the death of a dream for the millions of Europeans who have come to believe in the humanist vision for an open and free continent, not to mention the possibility of transcending its dark history of nationalism and bloodshed.

However, the fierce debate surrounding the current migration crisis goes beyond just the survival of the Schengen Agreement, as central an issue as that may be. It also goes beyond squabbles over refugee quotas or equitable sharing of the financial burden of dealing with the crisis. I would argue that it is really a debate about what kind of Europe emerges when, decades from now, this crisis is over. Will Western European countries survive relatively intact, or will they be unrecognizable from the open, pluralistic, and to some extent welcoming liberal democracies that emerged from the ashes of the World War II. Will they become insular and hostile to the world's needy? What vision of Europe ultimately prevails will depend on what faction of European society wins the debate?

One faction, exemplified by the likes of Daniel Trilling, the British writer and editor of the magazine *New Humanist*, has described the current migration crisis in stark political and moral terms. "Either Europe will continue to militarize its borders and squabble over resettlement quotas of refugees as if they were toxic waste," he writes in an op-ed for *The Guardian*, "or we will find the courage and leadership to create a just asylum system where member states pull together to ensure that refugees are offered a basic standard of living wherever they arrive."[8] When I talk with him via Skype, Trilling tells me that there is a kind of collective amnesia, a need not to remember, or even worse, deny Europe's complicity in the current migration crisis.

"There is a strong moral argument," he says. "Europe, having built its wealth on the backs of people in other parts of the world, has a moral duty to help those people, particularly because they're fleeing situations that

European countries had a hand in creating."

Whether you consider African economic migrants or Middle Eastern refugees from Syria and Iraq or other conflict-laden locales, European powers have been intimately involved, often for their own enrichment, in shaping and reshaping the destinies of nations in large swaths of Africa and the Middle East. There is, to this crisis, an aspect of, to put it crudely, "chickens coming home to roost." Leaving aside the destructive colonial legacies of countries such as Italy, France, and most of all Britain, there is a persuasive argument that many of the top migrant producing countries—Eritrea, Somalia, Libya, Syria, Afghanistan, and Iraq— are in the situation they are in largely due to recent foreign policy blunders by the West, including European powers. Trilling says he is often bemused by the tenor of the migration debate in Britain and the continent at large. "There is a sense in Europe as if there is no prior connection between us and the refugees who are arriving," he says. "The impression given by critics [of migrants] is that they're coming here to exploit us, when historically, it has been the opposite. . . . There are [political and economic] processes that have been going on far longer than the current crisis."

While traveling around Italy and France and speaking to some of the locals, I noticed a certain cognitive dissonance that allows many liberal, middle-class Europeans to distance their high standards of living from the source of their affluence. Many European countries continue to sell billions of euros worth of weapons to various countries in Africa and the Middle East where violence has compelled thousands to flee their countries. For instance, it recently became known that the UK government "signed off £3.3bn of arms exports to Saudi Arabia in the first year of the country's bombardment of Yemen."[9] Saudi Arabia has been using these weapons against Yemeni rebels—all too often killing civilians—even though their

British-made cluster bombs are banned by the Convention on Cluster Munitions, an international treaty to which the United Kingdom is party. The civil war in Yemen, which has been raging since 2015, has produced a dire refugee crisis. Over two million Yemenis have been forced to flee their homes, according to UNHCR figures, and although most remain internally displaced or have fled to neighboring countries, a small number have sought refuge in Europe. Still, many British politicians, especially those in the current Conservative government, have no qualms telling Yemini refugees trying to enter Britain that they are not welcome.

Much closer to the homes of everyday citizens, much of the wine, produce, and cheese sold and enjoyed across Europe for relatively cheap prices come from the hard labor of illegal migrants working in exploitive conditions on farms all over Southern Europe. Still, popular support for anti-migrant politicians is rising across the continent. Clearly, there is a serious disconnect in rationale. It is high time for Europeans to incorporate certain uncomfortable truths into their self-conception and calculations in trying to find just resolutions to the ongoing crisis. The people fleeing across the sea in rickety boats are not complete strangers. As Trilling tells me, these migrants are "coming with their own stories about how Europe was already playing a very intimate part in their lives and their parents and their grandparent's lives even before they arrived here."

On the other side of the current migration debate in Europe are people who view themselves as besieged. Philippe Legrain, the economist and author of the book *Immigrants: Your Country Needs Them* sums up their position disparagingly: "The barbarians have breached the gates. Europe is being overrun. Our civilization and our prosperity are at risk."[10] He goes on to make a case for the need to integrate migrants. But for every Trilling or Legrain, there are many others who would like to see the walls go up. One of the most prominent voices in this camp is the author Christopher Caldwell, who argues in his column for the *Weekly Standard* that "Europe must now provide the force to defend its own border. Europe does not need to indulge in brutality, only to show resolve."[11]

In 2009, Caldwell famously asked if it was possible to have "the same Europe with different people in it?"[12] Unsurprisingly, his answer was a resounding "no." For intellectuals like Caldwell, the debate is not so much about whether Europe can or should take in so many asylum seekers. The concern is what kind of Europe there will be when all these "masses from the south," as he calls them, settle down and have children. For Caldwell and others, that means the death of Europe, at least as conservatives currently conceive it. What worries them the most, it seems, are long-term demographic shifts due to mass migration coupled with decreasing birthrates among Europeans. It goes without saying that not all Europeans who are against migration are motivated by racism and xenophobia. There are millions of Europeans who do sympathize with the plight of refugees and migrants but their sympathies seem to be outweighed by an increasing sense that the continent is under a demographic assault. This is a potentially explosive populist sentiment that could usher into power right-wing ideologues such as Marine Le Pen and Geert Wilders when France and the Netherlands go to the polls in 2017. Whether watching the news or reading the papers in Europe, I am astonished by the disconnect between the lives of the migrants I encountered and the way immigrants generally are portrayed in the media. It was shocking, but not particularly surprising, for example, when Britain's controversial tabloid columnist Katie Hopkins referred to migrants in one of her columns as "cockroaches." Nor is it surprising to hear Marine Le Pen, the leader of France's National Front, or Matteo Salvini, leader of

Italy's Northern League, regularly make direct links between migrants and terrorism despite very little evidence connecting new migrants to international terrorism.

Increasingly, however, mainstream European politicians like Britain's former Prime Minister David Cameron have used disturbing—some call it "coded"—language to describe refugees and migrants. Cameron famously came under fire for referring to them as "a swarm of people."

There is a certain language being used in Europe and increasingly in America these days. Its intent seems to be undermining the idea that economic migrants are just like the rest of us: people who desire the same things we all do. As Mathew Carr reminds us in his book *Fortress Europe: Dispatches from a Gated Continent*, "history is filled with examples in which unwanted people have been driven 'beyond human boundary' in an attempt to preserve or confirm the character of the state or the collective identities of those who live inside their borders."[13] In the current European migration debate, there seems to be a concerted attempt to render migrants somehow mysterious. They are being "othered" as if human history has not been made up of people leaving their homelands in search of better lives, as if migration has not been a foundation upon which much of human progress rests. "Othered" as if human migration has not animated the ambitions and destinies of entire civilizations; as if migrants are risking less when they risk their lives.

It is my last day in Calais and I visit the camp one more time to say goodbye to Ahmed. He agrees to show me the highway where he managed to sneak into the truck on that November morning, was caught by the police and had his wrist broken. We walk past many shops, past the colorful sign that reads "Welcome to the City," and past the ten or so CRS police vans parked under the bridge that acts as the camp's de facto gate. We follow the ramp that leads to the highway, but that is as far as we are allowed to go. The tall, menacing fence that stands before us makes it clear that the highway is off limits. That fence is a physical reminder of the gulf between the harsh lives the residents lead within the camp and the promised land that exists just on the other side of the water. As we stare into the distant horizon, past the fences and the highway in the direction of "freedom," Ahmed tells me he has relatives in London who are waiting for him. Hope, Ahmed says, is what keeps him going—hope that nothing he has endured to get to Calais will be in vain.

One of the paradoxes of camp life is found in the constant interplay between present hopelessness and hopefulness for the future. Ahmed tells me then that he will try his luck in the Jungle for another six or seven months; if, by then, he has not succeeded in sneaking into England, he will be forced to reassess his dreams, perhaps seeking asylum in Finland, where he has a few friends. I ask Ahmed what he plans to do in London if he gets there. He tells me that all he ever wanted was to find a good job, send some money back home to his parents and nine siblings, and maybe—if things went well—start a family of his own. As I listen to Ahmed talk about his hopes and dreams, I am struck by just how ordinary they are. There is no denying that the current migration crisis unfolding in Europe is extraordinary. But take away the extraordinary numbers of refugees and migrants marching across the continent—take away the daring acts of desperation, strip away the hyper-polarized politics—and what's left are ordinary people with the most ordinary yearnings: safety, free-dom, jobs. The basic stuff of life.

Dusk comes without warning and casts every-thing in a soft, mauve light. We amble back to the camp. Before Ahmed and I go our separate ways, he allows me to snap a few photographs of him under the highway bridge where the camp begins. We exchange a quick hug and a promise to stay in touch. I watch him walk toward the

camp, his broken hand still in a cast. Moments later, I lose sight of him.

———

Many months have passed since I said farewell to Ahmed at the gate of the Calais Jungle. Since then, the camp has been demolished and all the residents who used to call it home have been scattered all over France, the friendships, and communities they created destroyed along with the tents that once sheltered them. I have tried several times to contact Ahmed through the email account he gave me, but I have yet to receive a reply. I have also searched for him on Facebook, but there seems to be no sign of his existence. At times, Ahmed feels like a ghost I somehow willed into being.

As I go about my daily life half a world away, I often wonder what has become of him. In these fleeting thoughts, I imagine him in a new life. Maybe he managed to make it to London after all, and is living the dream that had sustained him throughout his long journey. It is highly unlikely, but I find comfort in the fantasy. In another scenario, he is living in Helsinki where he told me he might travel to if his efforts in the camp proved futile. But in all likelihood, Ahmed, like most of the former residents of the Calais Jungle, is now living in a temporary migrant center somewhere in France—a fate he always dreaded. Wherever he is, I hope he is safe. I hope he has at last found the stability and sense of home that has eluded him almost all his life. I hope he finds the cherished, fragile dreams that propelled him so far away from home.

Ahmed, December 28, 2015. Photo by Hassan Ghedi Santur.

1   Matthias Blamont. *Clearance of Calais Jungle Camp Accomplished, French Prefect Says.* Reuters, October 26, 2016.
2   Adam Nossiter. *Shouts Greet Migrants in the Streets of France: "We Don't Want Them."* New York Times, October 25, 2016.
3   Amelia Gentleman. *Refugees Take to Hiding in Northern France after Calais Camp Demolished.* The Guardian, November 6, 2016.
4   Ingrid Melander. *More Migrants Pitch Tents on Paris Streets as Calais Camp Shuts.* Reuters, October 29, 2016.
5   Stephanie Kirchgaessner. *We Were Abandoned: Migrants Tell of Suffering in Italy's Private Shelters.* The Guardian, November 26, 2015.
6   Alex De Waal. *Africa's $700 Billion Problem Waiting to Happen.* Foreign Policy, March 17, 2016.
7   *Libya is Full of Cruelty: Stories of Abduction, Sexual Violence, and Abuse from Migrants and Refugees.* Amnesty International, 2015. The report can be accessed on line at: http://www.amnesty.eu/content/assets/Reports_and_Briefings_2015/Libya_is_full_of_cruelty.pdf
8   Daniel Trilling. *Europe Could Solve the Migrant Crisis—If It Wanted.* The Guardian, July 31, 2015.
9   Rob Merrick. *Theresa May Claims Selling Arms to Saudi Arabia Helps "Keep People on the Streets of Britain Safe."* The Independent, September 7, 2016.
10 Philippe Legrain. *Europe Needs to Let the Migrants In.* Foreign Policy, August 24, 2015.
11 Christopher Caldwell. *Waves from the South.* Weekly Standard, September 21, 2015.
12 Christopher Caldwell. *Reflections on the Revolution in Europe: Immigration, Islam, and the West.* Anchor, 2009.
13 Matthew, Carr. *Fortress Europe: Dispatches from a Gated Continent.* New Print, 2012.

Acknowledgements

I am an immigrant. In 1989, my family left Somalia to escape the worsening political situation in the country that eventually led to a bloody, twenty-year civil war. My life has been made immeasurably better by migration. As a result, I have always been fascinated by the plight of refugees and migrants and what drives people to upend their lives and migrate to unknown lands.

Working on *Maps of Exile* has been a labor of love to which so many kind, smart, talented people have contributed. My sincere thanks to Alessandro Bisogni, Bhakti Shringarpure, Michael Bronner, Michael Busch, Gareth Davies, Léopold Lambert, Alexander Stille, Lauren B. Davis, Lara Pawson, Nadifa Mohamed, Nicholas Lemann, Tali Woodward, Sieraaj Ahmed, Sowmiya Ashok, Ottavio Balzano, Daniel Trilling, Andrea Costa and many more.

I am also grateful to the generous travel grant I received from The Correspondents Fund which made it possible for me to travel to Europe for a month to report this story. Above all, I would like thank Ahmed Ibrahim Sa'eed, Torey Ibrahim, Immanuel Ufuku, Bushar Ahmed, Hassan Abdullah, Ahmed Omar, Kamal and the many other African men I met in Naples, Rome, and Calais, and who generously shared their stories with me. One of the things I love most about being a journalist is when people invite me into their homes, in the case of the Jungle, their tents, and entrust me with their stories. I am always humbled by their trust in me. It is a privilege and a responsibility I cherish. I hope I have succeeded in faithfully and accurately telling their stories and experiences.

The Gift by Alfredo Jaar, 2016. Public Intervention, Basel. Courtesy the artist, New York.

Refugees: A Starter Syllabus

Literature

Akpan, Uwem. *Say You're One of Them.* Thorndike, Me.: Center Point Pub., 2009. Print.

Balakian, Peter. *Black Dog of Fate: A Memoir.* New York: Basic, 2009. Print.

Bulawayo, NoViolet. *We Need New Names.* Harare: Weaver, 2014. Print.

Danticat, Edwidge. *Breath, Eyes, Memory.* New York, NY: Soho, 2015. Print.

Danticat, Edwidge. *Krik? Krak!* New York: Soho, 2015. Print.

Diome, Fatou, Lulu Norman, and Ros Schwartz. *The Belly of the Atlantic.* London: Serpent's Tail, 2006. Print.

Eggers, Dave. *What Is the What: The Autobiography of Valentino Achak Deng: A Novel.* London: Penguin, 2008. Print.

Farah, Cristina Ali. *Little Mother: A Novel.* Bloomington, IN: Indiana UP, 2011. Print.

Hailu, Gebreyesus, Ghirmai Negash, and Laura Chrisman. *The Conscript: A Novel of Libya's Anticolonial War.* Athens, OH: Ohio UP, 2013. Print.

Hosseini, Khaled. *The Kite Runner.* New York: Riverhead, 2013. Print.

Kahal, Abu Bakr, and Charis Bredin. *African Titanics.* London: Darf, 2014. Print.

Kanafani, Ghassan, and Hilary Kilpatrick. *Men in the Sun & Other Palestinian Stories.* Boulder: Lynne Rienner, 1999.

Lalami, Laila. *Hope And Other Dangerous Pursuits.* Fez: Moroccan Cultural Studies Centre, 2008. Print.

Mengestu, Dinaw. *The Beautiful Things That Heaven Bears.* New York: Riverhead, 2008. Print.

Mezlekia, Nega. *Notes from the Hyena's Belly: An Ethiopian Boyhood.* New York: Picador USA, 2002. Print.

Sebald, W. G., and Michael Hulse. *The Emigrants.* New York: New Directions, 2016. Print.

Selvadurai, Shyam. *The Hungry Ghosts.* London: Telegram, 2016. Print.

Umutesi, Marie Béatrice. *Surviving the Slaughter: The Ordeal of a Rwandan Refugee in Zaire.* Madison: U of Wisconsin, 2004. Print.

Poetry

Adonis, Mahmoud Darwish, Samih Al-Qasim, and Ali Ahmad Said. *Victims of a Map: A Bilingual Anthology of Arabic Poetry.* London: Saqi, 2005. Print.

Alyan, Hala. *Salt Houses.* Boston: Houghton Mifflin Harcourt, 2017. Print.

Brecht, Bertolt. "On the Suicide of the Refugee W.B." Red Wedge. N.p., 05 Oct. 2015. Web. 16 Apr. 2017.

Darwish, Mahmoud, and Munir Akash. *State of Siege.* Syracuse, N.Y: Jusoor and Syracuse UP, 2010. Print.

Emmerich, Karen, Edmund Keeley, and Yiannis Ritsos. *Diaries of Exile.* Brooklyn, NY: Archipelago, 2013. Print.

Khaleed, Jazra. "Translation Tuesday: The War Is Coming by Jazra Khaleed." *Guardian.* Guardian News and Media, 10 Jan. 2017. Web. 16 Apr. 2017.

Shire, Warsan. *Teaching My Mother How to Give Birth.* N.p.: Lightning Source, 2014. Print.

Film

4.1 Miles. Dir. Daphne Matziaraki. 2017. Film.

Fire at Sea (Fuocoammare). Dir. Gianfranco Rosi. 01 Distribution, 2016. Film.

Lamerica. Dir. Gianni Amelio. Perf. Enrico Lo Verso and Michele Placido. New Yorker Films, 1994. Film.

La pirogue. Dir. Moussa Touré. Perf. Abasse Ndione, Éric Névé, David Bouchet. 2012. Film.

Mediterranea. Dir. Jonas Carpignano. 2015, Film.

The Land Between. Dir. David Fedele. 2014. Film.

Theory

Agamben, Giorgio. *Homo Sacer: Sovereign Power and Bare Life.* Stanford, CA: Stanford University Press, 1998. Print.

Agaben, Giorgio. *State of Exception.* Chicago: University Of Chicago Press, 2005. Print.

Agier, Michael. *On the Margins of the World: The Refugee Experience Today.* Cambridge, UK: Polity, 2008. Print.

Agier, Michael. *Managing the Undesirables: Refugee Camps and Humanitarian Government.* Cambridge, UK: Polity, 2011. Print.

Ahmed, Sara. "Home and Away: Narratives of Migration and Estrangement." *International Journal of Cultural Studies*, 2, vol. 3 (1999): 329-347. Print.

Arendt, Hannah. *Origins of Totalitarianism.* New York: Harcourt, Brace, and Jovanovich, 1973. Print.

Arendt, Hannah. "We Refugees," in *Altogether Elsewhere,* Marc Robinson (ed.). New York: Harvest, 1996. Print.

Bauer, Wolfgang and Stanislav Krupar. *Crossing the Sea: With Syrians on the Exodus to Europe.* High Wycombe, UK: Other Stories Press, 2016. Print.

Bauman, Zygmunt. *Liquid Times: Living in an Age of Uncertainty.* London: Polity, 2006. Print.

Bauman, Zygmunt. *Strangers at Our Door.* London: Polity, 2016. Print.

Benhabib, Syla. *The Rights of Others: Aliens, Residents, Citizens.* Cambridge, UK: Cambridge University Press, 2004. Print.

Benhabib, Seyla. *Another Cosmopolitanism.* Oxford: Oxford University Press, 2006. Print.

Betts, Alexander, Gil Loescher, and James Milner. *The United Nations High Commissioner for Refugees (UNHCR): The Politics and Practice of Refugee Protection.* London: Routledge, 2012.

Brah, Avtar. *Cartograhies of Diaspora: Contesting Identities.* London: Routledge, 1996.

Braidotti, Rosi. *Nomadic Subjects: Embodiment and Sexual Difference in Contemporary Feminist Theory.* New York: Columbia University Press, 1994.

Butler, Judith. *Precarious Life: The Powers of Mourning and Violence.*

London: Verso, 2006. Print.

Coundouriotis, Eleni. "In flight: The refugee experience and human rights narrative." *The Routledge Companion to Literature and Human Rights* edited by McClennan, Sophia A. & Moore, Alexandra Schultheis. Routledge, 2015.

Dillon, Michael. "The Sovereign and the Stranger," in Jenny Edkins, Nalina Persram and Véronique Pin-Fent (eds.) *Sovereignty and Subjectivity.* London: Lynne Rienner, 1999..

Dhingra, Leela. "La Vie en rose," in Kate Pullinger (ed.) *Border Lines: Stories of Exile and Home.* New York: Serpent's Tail, 1993
.

Evans, Kate. *Threads: From the Refugee Crisis.* London: Verso, 2017. Print.

Farah, Nuruddin. *Yesterday, Tomorrow: Voices from the Somali Diaspora.* London: Cassell, 2000. Print.

Fassin, Didier. *Humanitarian Reason: A Moral History of the Present.* Berkeley and Los Angeles: University of California Press, 2012. Print.

Fiddian-Qasmiiyeh, Elena, Gil Loescher, Katy Long, and Nando Sigona (eds.). *The Oxford Handbook of refugee and Forced Migration Studies.* New York: Oxford University Press, 2016.

Ganguly, Keya. "Migrant Identities, Personal Memory and the Construction of Self." *Cultural Studies* 6 (1992): 27-51. Print.

Gündogdu, Ayten. *Rightlessness in an Age of Rights: Hannah Arendt and the Contemporary Struggles of Migrants.* Oxford: Oxford University Press, 2015. Print.

Hirsch, Mariann. *Family Frames: Photography, Narratives and Postmemory.* Cambridge, MA: Harvard University Press, 1997. Print.

Hirsch, Mariann. *Generation of Postmemory: Writing and Visual Culture after the Holocaust.* New York: Columbia University Press, 2012. Print.

Holton, Jan. *Longing for Home: Forced Displacement and Postures of Hospitality.* New Haven, CT: Yale University Press, 2016. Print.

Holzer, Elizabeth Holzer. *The Concerned Women of Buduburam: Refugee Activists and Humanitarian Dilemmas.* Ithaca, NY: Cornell, 2015. Print.

Jones, Reece. *Violent Borders: Refugees and the Right to Move.* London: Verso, 2016. Print.

Kingsley, Patrick. *The New Odyssey: The Story of the Twenty-first Century Refugee Crisis.* New York: Liveright, 2017. Print.

Mannick, Lynda. *Migration by Boat: Discourses of Trauma, Exclusion and Survival.* New York and Oxford: Berghahn Books, 2016. Print.

McConnachie, "Camps of Containment: A Genealogy of the Refugee Camp." *Humanity: An International Journal of Human Rights, Humanitarianism and Development* 7, vol. 3 (2016): 397-412.

McCourt, Frank. *Angela's Ashes: A Memoir.* New York: Scribner, 1999. Print.

Monk, Daniel Bertrand and Andrew Herschel. "The New Universalism: Refuges and Refugees Between Global History and Voucher Humanitarianism." *Grey Room*, 61 (2015): 71-80. Print.

Olivier, Kelly. *Carceral Humanitarianism: Logics of Refugee Detention.* Minneapolis: University of Minnesota Press, 2017. Print.

Parekh, Serena. *Refugees and the Ethics of Forced Displacement.* London: Routledge, 2016. Print.

Persram, Nalina. "In My Father's House are Many Mansions: The Nation and Post-Colonial Desire," in Heidi Mirza (ed.) *Black British Feminism*. London: Routledge, 1996. Print.

Rawlence, Ben. *City of Thorns*. New York: Macmillan, 2017. Print.

al-Sabouni, Marwa, *The Battle for Home: The Vision of a Young Architect in Syria*. London: Thames and Hudson, 2016. Print.

Said, Edward. *After the Last Sky: Palestinian Lives*. New York: Columbia University Press, 1999. Print.

Santur, Hassan Ghedi. *Maps of Exile*. New York: Warscapes, 2017. E-book.

Stamselberg, Nadja (ed.). *Breaching Borders: Art, Migrants and the Metaphor of Waste*. London: I.B. Taurus, 2014. Print.

Tickton, Miriam. "Humanitarianism's History of the Singular," *Grey Room* 61 (2015): 81-86. Print.

United Nations Convention and Protocol Relating to the Status of Refugees. Available online at.

Weiss, Thomas and Michael Barnett. *Humanitarianism in Question: Politics, Power, Ethics*. Ithaca, NY: Cornell University Press, 2008. Print.

Yazbek, Samar. *The Crossing: My Journey to the Shattered Heart of Syria*. London, Ebury Press, 2016. Print.

Zizek, Slavoj. *Against the Double Blackmail: Refugees, Terror and Other Troubles with Neighbors*. New York: Penguin, 2017. Print.

Zolberg, Aristide, Astri Suhrke, and Sergio Aguayo. *Escape for Violence: The Refugee Crisis in the Developing World*. Oxford: Oxford University Press, 1992. Print.

Art

Shadows of the Wanderer by Ana Maria Pacheco, Chichester Cathedral. The Royal Chantry, Cathedral Cloisters, Chichester PO19 1PX, UK, 2016.

The Kindertransport Commemorative Statue by Frank Meisler and Arie Oviada, Outside Liverpool Street Station, London, 2006

Grace Reef by Jason DeCaires Taylor, Molinere Underwater Sculpture Park - and underwater museum. Caribbean sea off the west coast of Grenada, West Indies, 2006 and Museo Atlantico Off the coast of Lanzarote, Spain, February 25, 2016

Law of the Journey by Ai Weiwei, National Gallery in Prague, Czech Republic, March 16, 2017-January 7, 2018

Safety Orange Swimmers (S.O.S) by Ann Hirsch and Jeremy Angier, Boston's Fort Point Section, October 2016

Inflatable Refugee by Schellekens & Peleman, Travelling Venice, Italy, Helsingor, Copenhagen, Uppsala, Vejle, Mechelen, 2017

Transition/Evacuation by Khadim Ali and Sher Ali, Milani Gallery, Woolloongabba QLD 4102, Australia, July 26, 2014 - August 9, 2014

The Box by Barthélémy Toguo, Pippy Houldsworth Gallery in London, September 4 - October 3, 2015

Urban Requiem by Barthélémy Toguo, Venice Biennale, 2015

Road for Exile by Barthélémy Toguo, The Devilish Human Temptations, Mario Mauroner Contemporary Art Vienna, Austria, 2008

God Sets the Course for the Ship and Not the Captain by Shahpour Pouyan, London's Copperfield Gallery in an exhibition entitled "History Travels at Different Speeds," 2008-Present

Erasure by Dinh Q. Lê, Several locations, September 2011

Immigrants by Popi Nicolaou, Giorgos Mouskis, Christos Hambiaouris, Christos Charalambous, Annita Yianni, Panayiotis Panayiotou, Nikoletta Elia, Loukia Varna, and Vasilis Vasiliou, Saatchi Gallery in London, March 3 - 9, 2016

Vertigo Sea by John Akomfrah, Venice Biennale. Arnolfini in the UK: Lisson Gallery New York 2015 and 2016.

Residenzpflicht (Duty of Residence) by Invisible Borders, On loan in several locations.

Ghost by Kader Attia, Pompidou Center in Paris, France and Saatchi Gallery London, 2007

La Colonie by Kader Attia, Paris, France, October 17, 2016

Regarding the Pain of Others by Khaled Barakeh, New Frankfurt International—Solid Sign, Frankfurter Kunstverein, Frankfurt, 2013.

Transmigration by Khaled Barakeh, Staedelschule, Frankfurt, Germany, 2012.

Insecurities: Tracing Displacement and Shelter by Sean Anderson and Arièle Dionne-Krosnick, MoMA in NYC, October 1, 2016–January 22, W

The Gift by Alfredo Jaar, Art Basel: Parcours, Basel, Switzerland, 2016

Sheddings by I.B. Itso, Galleri Nicolai Wallner, 2016

The Mapping Journey Project, Bouchra Khalili, MoMA brochure and also at Lisson Gallery, United Kingdom, 2008-2011

The Constellation Series by Bouchra Khalili, Färgfabriken Konsthall, 2011

Contributors

Ali Jimale Ahmed is a Somali poet and scholar. He is Chair and Professor of Comparative Literature at Queens College and the CUNY Graduate Center. His books include *The Invention of Somalia, Daybreak is Near: Literature, Clans and the Nation-state in Somalia, Fear is a Cow* and *Diaspora Blues*.

Mario Badagliacca is a documentary photographer and photojournalist from Italy. His work has been published in *La Repubblica, Corriere della Sera, Left/ L'Unità^Le nouvelle Observateur, Radio RAI3, National Geographic, Warscapes, Mondadori* and *Pellegrini*.

Ana Dana Beroš is an architect, curator, editor and educator. She is the co-founder of ARCHIsquad - Division for Architecture with Conscience, Think Space, Future Architecture and Urgent Architecture.

Mary Bosworth is Professor of Criminology at the University of Oxford. She is Assistant Director of the Centre for Criminology and Director of Border Criminologies, an interdisciplinary research group focusing on the intersections between criminal justice and border control. She is the author of *The US Federal Prison System, Explaining U.S. Imprisonment* and *Inside Immigration Detention*.

Jehan Bseiso is a Palestinian poet, researcher and aid worker. Her poetry has been published in *Warscapes, The Electronic Intifada,* and *Mada Masr,* among others. Bseiso is co-editing *Making Mirrors,* a new anthology by, for and about refugees.

Veruska Cantelli is a writer, translator and contributing editor for *Warscapes*. She is Assistant Professor of Interdisciplinary Studies at Champlain College.

Edwidge Danticat is an award-winning writer of Haitian descent. Her books include *Breath, Eyes, Memory, Krik? Krak! The Dew Breaker, The Farming of Bones* and *Claire of the Sea Lighti,* among several others.

Boubacar Boris Diop is a Senegalese writer who writes in French and Wolof. His novels include *Murambi: The Book of Bones, Kaveena, The Knight and his Shadow* and *Doomi Golo: The Hidden Notebooks,* among others.

Ismail Einashe is a British-Somali journalist who has reported for the *Guardian, Prospect Magazine, Warscapes, Mail & Guardian, The Nation, BBC* and *The Atlantic*.

Mujtaba Jalali, born in Iran to Afghan refugee parents, was persecuted and arrested in Iran for his work as a documentary photographer and journalist. He fled Iran to Europe over land and sea via Turkey, ultimately winning asylum in the Netherlands. He has produced a series of photographs documenting a year he spent housed with other refugees in three different former Dutch prisons.

Léopold Lambert is an architect and writer based in Paris. He is the founder and editor-in-chief of *The Funambulist Magazine*.

Maaza Mengiste is an Ethiopian-American writer and photographer. She is the author of *Beneath the Lion's Gaze* and is Lecturer of Creative Writing in the Lewis Center for the Arts at Princeton University.

Hassan Ghedi Santur was born in Somalia and migrated to Canada as a teenager. He is a journalist as well as a fiction writer. His debut novel is *Something Remains*.

Chika Unigwe is a Nigerian writer who lives in the United States. She is the author of *Born in Nigeria, A Rainbow for Dinner, Thinking of Angel* and *Night Dancer,* among others.